G000140349

Josh Logan is an aspiring author, bringing many ideologies and new storytelling impressions to the forefront of fiction. He intends to bring many more works to bookshelves, provoking thoughts among readers, encouraging them each to have a unique interpretation of his work. Josh hopes you enjoy the nature of all his works and incoherent mumblings on paper.

Josh Logan

THE MAN OF 100 CURSES

AUSTIN MACAULEY PUBLISHERS™

LONDON • CAMBRIDGE • NEW YORK • SHARJAH

Copyright © Josh Logan (2021)

The right of Josh Logan to be identified as author of this work has been asserted by the author in accordance with section 77 and 78 of the Copyright, Designs and Patents Act 1988.

All rights reserved. No part of this publication may be reproduced, stored in a retrieval system, or transmitted in any form or by any means, electronic, mechanical, photocopying, recording, or otherwise, without the prior permission of the publishers.

Any person who commits any unauthorised act in relation to this publication may be liable to criminal prosecution and civil claims for damages.

This is a work of fiction. Names, characters, businesses, places, events, locales, and incidents are either the products of the author's imagination or used in a fictitious manner. Any resemblance to actual persons, living or dead, or actual events is purely coincidental.

A CIP catalogue record for this title is available from the British Library.

ISBN 9781398412736 (Paperback)
ISBN 9781398412743 (ePub e-book)

www.austinmacauley.com

First Published (2021)
Austin Macauley Publishers Ltd
25 Canada Square
Canary Wharf
London
E14 5LQ

Chapter 1
The Journey

Tipping the bottle over the fulcrum point, my eyes narrowed to observe the last drop of water edging closer to my dry and cracked lips. I was miles from the nearest village and out in the moors – the weather was vicious and unforgiving. At times, months could pass and not a cloud could be seen, yet on others, rain could fall, drowning the land into an endless murky swamp. The knowledge that the nearby village was the fabled home to the hag of the east woods drove me. Stumbling over the roots and weeds, the grass weaving over my weathered boots, I struggled yet one foot always seemed to replace the other and I moved on. I was John Sawyer, son of the Sawyer Carpenters Family in Scotland. I still remember the anxious look in my father's eyes and the wobble in his voice as he told me, word for word.

"My son, I must ask of you that of which I would never ask even the lowly beggars of our country. Here, you see I have used the skills of our family, passed down from my father and his father before him, to craft this." And in my infant hands he placed a small wood carving of a rune pendant. "Now, down in England, there lives a witch among the plains. Some say she speaks to the skies and whispers poems of darkness to the lakes. She requires this rune to pay off a debt to aid her in her dark magics. Son, you must take it to her."

The sudden feeling of relief entered my mind when, as I clambered over a boggy mound, I saw a faint cloud in the sky. At first I believed my eyes to be deceiving me, for in these parts deception and lies was common amongst the travellers, the wildlife and the land. I stumbled towards it, this time at a pace I hadn't ran in weeks. Drops of sweat fell from the tip of my chin, now littered with stubble, interwoven and rugged yet surprisingly youthful. My father warned me of this place. As a child all the tales he told as he tucked me under the bed sheets were of the Wildlands and dangers of England. Tales that used to somehow find their way to invade my dreams, causing abrupt awakenings in a puddle of sweat and piss. One thing was for certain, if one were looking for safety in the wildlands, they would look for the villages that rain salt water. I can recall my father telling me how the salt water was the tears from an ancient god, and that repulsed the dark entities that wandered the fields and hills of England, keeping them away. The Burncorn village was a pleasant site to see, the keep in the middle home to generations of noble bloodlines. The area seemingly began to dissipate around the edges, with the smaller huts homing the less fortunate. My bloodshot eyes darted around, to see the inhabitants pause their farming, trading, and drinking to glare back at me, a foreigner. I limped over to a farmer, dragging my exhausted body over the muddy damp floor.

"Hell do you wan'?" he stated, scratching the flea's residing in his grey beard.

"Sir, the hag from the East Wood. Tales of her kin reached borders of my country. I must speak with her."

The farm man proceeded to frown at me, before throwing his hand out to shake mine. His hand was tough skinned, that of which only a farmer could have. Some say the farmers in these parts could catch a sword mid swing, and it still couldn't break the callous on their hands. Back when the civil war plagued these parts most of the farmers were drafted for war leaving their land and livestock, to kill and draw blood from men who could be neighbours or family.

"The names, Yen. Yer goin' to need a guide. Someone who knows the East Wood. People get lost in there and by the time they next see sunlight, their bout to turn 90." He grinned.

"Yes, yes of course. I am John. I have been journeying since the last full moon, and I'm sure you know the journey here was no easy task. Feed me and clothe me. I will pay you in pure silver from the mountains of my country."

He grunted an unsatisfied grunt and gestured me to follow him. The route back to his shack was eye opening. Seeing children covered in dirt and mud and veterans drunk still seeing the after mirage of war. There was a deep sense of underlying concern for the barbaric, and inhuman conditions of the villagers of Burncorn.

"The nobleman of this village?" I enquired.

"Of Burncorn? Sir Nash? He don't leave his bloody big castle. He's a knight too ya know. Came back after the war, lost his brothers and father I heard and shacked himself up. No one's seen him in years."

The castle was made of white marble and among the village of nothing, it was a bright beacon of hope for some, and for others, it was a dark mockery of what they had become. Yens shack was little more than the other villagers had. Dimly lit by a centre fire, the shadows danced on the walls that were cluttered with trinkets and other mystical objects.

"You been collecting for a while?" I asked turning to Yen, who was cooking rat skewers over the tongues of the flame.

"Well. Can't be too safe around the wildlands. Those ones your lookin' at there, got em blessed by an exorcist who passed through a few moons ago. Said he was the one who cast out the ghost of the drowned man from the lake in the East Woods. After losing my dear, Amelia, can't be too safe."

At this moment in time, his demeanour changed. He was no longer a rough farmer, but a broken veteran. A man who lost someone, his family.

"Sit, foreigner. I got a story for you."

I sat as he passed me a bowl that was filled to the brim with rat meat and a brine that smelled of lavender, picked from the fresh green fields surrounding Burncorn. He went on.

"There was once a man. A young and clever man, prospect of the village. They say he was such a talented smith, that royalty begged him to create jewels and crowns for their heads and their heirs. The man grew and wedded a gorgeous young woman, and they bore a son, prophesised to become like his father. Fear struck the father's heart, for disease writhed through the towns and villages. The illness grew and with it and death was invited to snuff the flame of life from hundreds of innocent people. Eventually the inevitable took place, and the sickness inhabited the mother of the child. The father, grief stricken and selfish, began searching for an answer. He ventured out to the wilderness and begged to the sky for a cure or a power to save the one he loved. Before him stood a hunched being wrapped in black cloth. Rumours infected the tale at this point for no one knows truly what happened that night but from that point on the father had become efficient in dark arts, alchemy, and the sorts. He sought after his lover and calling on the dark magic, she was healed. Outraged, by the father's coalition with the unknown being, and his use of the dark powers to save his family and deny death, the village elders banished him and his son for bringing years of plague and famine to the land. And so, they wondered. And where they went, hunger, thirst and insanity ensued. They wondered out to the moors, far enough that the stars began to change, and the land became foreign. The elongated grass and bushes gripped at their cloaks, and the trees swayed from them as they too felt the curse the two gents bared. They survived a while, however the dark magic flowing through the veins of the father could only sustain the two of them for so long. They sought water for the demon of thirst sat on their shoulder, giving them visions of ponds and rivers that would cure them. Then, they envisioned the infamous well. Stumbling towards it, the father, caring for his son, hurled the rusted iron bucket into the shadowy depths before calling it back up seeing it filled to the brim with the black tinted liquid. The son relieved drank deeply from it, nourishing him fulfilling him ridding the demon of thirst. However, one demon was replaced by another one. Veins protruded from the boy's neck, and crimson blood seeped from his eyes. Convulsing and tensing, his father held him, tears streaming from his face as the boy became laced with streams of blood which was soaked up by the grounds of the moors and eaten by the greenery which inhabited the area.

Death had claimed the son too, as he held hands with his mother and joined her in the abyss of the void. Anger flowed through the father. Loss had become a familiar friend to him, although it was not one he wanted. The most unwanted and unkind friend. He stood over the lifeless body of his son all the features of him; his laugh, his smile and his ambition all claimed by this bewitched well. Furious he called upon all the dark powers forcefully bestowed upon him. Calling storms, fire, lightning and rain. He spoke in an ancient tongue only used by those affiliated with the depths of hell. He called curses upon the land. The land was to never come to fruition again. The sky was cursed with darkness, dark clouds and storms were to inhabit the land, and lightning was to strike down the aged trees taking their leaves and beauty and leaving them as a white, leafless trunk as ash fell to the ground. Lastly, spirits of those who the land claimed were cursed to wonder there, endlessly until the beast raises from the ocean to bring the end of time. As the night died and the sun rose in the east, the once home of the conjurer was no more than crisp burnt corpses and skeletons, their ghosts wondering the plains of the land in which the sorcerer's son passed. They would forever know the pain they caused the family. As for the father himself, no eye nor ear ever saw or heard him again. Sometimes, travellers stop at the inn in a nearby village, claiming to see a man, cloaked and his hands stained with blood, holding an iron bucket. Those who don't search for this man, come back with stories. Those who search for this man go 'missing'."

Listening to Yens rumours and tales triggered a deep fear inside me. I had heard similar tales from my father's mouth, but I knew not of the severity of the dark beings, ghosts, demons, and witchbloods that wandered the land. Voicing my concerns to Yen he gave me a look before leaning forward in his seat, his belly hindering his range of movement.

"Ah, come on, traveller. You ain't just gotta worry about the beings who walk among the wildlands. Nothing seem off about this land to you? Don't be naïve boy."

He began to get riled up, sipping from his rum bottle more frequently, slurring his words, and tears building in his aged blue eyes. The alcohol triggering repressed emotions, buried beneath years of guilt.

"I woke up this mornin' and vines from the tree just outside the village had wrapped around my neck! If I hadn't got up when the cock sang, I would be dead in the sack right now. The shadows on the land can't even begin to compare to what lies beneath."

When I was young, Father took me up to the tip of a mountain that was a few days trek from our home. The journey was in silence. Father was never the talking type, most of the words that left his mouth were expletives about the civil war, our king, or reprimanding me. At the peak, the winds were bitter and sharp. Listening carefully, you could hear it speaking to the sea, and the crashing waves would reply,

"Boy. This world we live in. Its full of beings filled with such darkness that would make even the darkest night seem like the brightest day. But listen. The most danger you will have to face doesn't come from these beings. They can be hurt with steel or flame and killed with psalms or verses. Utter words of magic and they could be trapped or cease to exist. The earth itself. That is your enemy. At some point in life you

11

may go places that the land doesn't want you to be. Run from it, boy."

Chapter 2

The East Woods

Amber leaves on the floor, fallen from the twigged fingers of winter branches, crunched under my boots. Hastily I followed closely behind Yen, close enough to smell the reluctant scent of hay bales and cow manure on his clothes. The crow flew overhead, its obscure shape blending with the blackness of the night sky. The night was calm, a sense of peace radiated from the star dotted abyss. On the horizon, the dull pink glow of the falling sun almost greeted the pale moon as it rose from the east. The peace was constant, yet on occasion was abruptly disturbed by the howling of a beast, or the unsettling cries of the dead. Yen crouched by a bramble bush at the tangent of a clearing in the woods and gestured me to his side.

"Are we close?" I muttered, my hot breath visible in the cold, obscuring my sight.

"Shut it, traveller," he snapped.

His eyes jolted to the clearing and mine naturally followed. Passing by there was a creature.

With fear in every fibre of his being Yen said, "Its Mr Brickenden."

The creature walked on its hind legs with fur like the spines of a hedgehog. Saliva dripped from the beast's jaws, his teeth, and claws sharp enough to rip through chainmail. Then an ear-piercing howl erupted and immediately cowering in fear, myself and Yen dived under the bramble bush. I covered my ears and scrunched my face; the noise rattled my teeth and I could feel my joints crunching and grinding. Silence fell, and the rustle of the trees was a sign that the beast had darted away, probably to hunt a kill.

"Mr Brickenden?" I asked. An unintentional tone of anger hit my voice. "You said this was a safe passage into the East Woods, one only the villagers knew of?"

"Yeah, and I meant it. Mr Brickenden helped us commoners build the Marble Castle back in the village. Poor guy. He made a mistake with the measurements, somethin' small. An error that could've been repaired by any man handy with a hammer and chisel. But the nobleman, Sir Nash, couldn't have that; oh no."

"What happened to him?"

"Sir Nash, the bastard, scanned the wildlands. Found himself a witch blooded woman. An expert in beast mutations. Mr Brickenden resides in the East Woods now."

Based on the information given to me from Yen and the evidence of the harrowing beast that once was Mr Brickenden, I had preconceived opinions on Sir Nash. I thought I recognised the family name somewhere. The Nash family was one of royal blood. However, their bloodline drew thin. Too far from the King Ichilla to be his heir. The Nash family were bitter. Driven to be cold and astringent because they would never sit on the throne of England. A family who thrived on the civil war, gaining fame for their ability to kill. Sir Nash of Burncorn, the man who resided in the Marble Castle, was bred to kill. Rumours flooded the villages of the wildlands that the fathers of Nash blood would purposely seek curses and runes to make them more formidable Knights, cursing their young within days of birth. My father always wanted me to be a knight. When I was but a child, he already had me smithing my first sword. I took pride in taking hammer to steel. The forge in Scotland was legendary. Myth says that the embers in the forge were lit by the last dragon alive, and the flames will die when the dragons one day return. When the sword was finally complete, it was far too large for me to wield. The leather wrapped handle felt good in my hands, my sweaty palms and coal stained skin. I was delirious with it. I had decided, through my father's encouragement, that I would one day be on the front lines of the royal guard, brandishing the black armour. And I would draw that sword and defeat the enemies of the country. It wasn't until the Civil war that the dream of achieving knighthood died. The Civil war destroyed the countries of England and Scotland. Some say King Ichilla was possessed by a devious spirit and that's what influenced his decision to go to war with the nobleman within the country. We will never know. Yen led the way deeper into the woods until the fractured branches blocked out the waning light of the moon.

"Ah, there she is," he said followed by a sigh of relief as we approached a mount in the forest.

It was a small hut, made from twigs, leaves and the sap from trees. Light emanated from the cracks in the walls, the flickering shadows of movement inside.

"She'll only see one person at once. You better hurry up."

I nodded and thanked Yen, slowly approaching what appeared to be a doorway. The door of the hut was splintered and old, with moss growing in the crevices of the carved wood which was being eaten by woodlouse. The door slowly cracked open, and I entered.

"Excuse me? I came to speak with the hag of East Woods?" I said.

My head swivelling like an owl analysing the 'home' of this Hag. Shelves that held jars which contained all sorts of mutated creatures and animals. Trinkets similar to the ones in Yens house engraved into the stick and stone walls of the hut.

"The hag of East Woods?" an echoing ethereal voice answered. "Is that what they call me these days?"

I turned for the door, fear getting the better of me, but I was greeted nose to nose with an old woman, her hair grey and black twisted and knotted. Her face covered with scars and boils. The detail that sent shivers down my spine was that her eyes were white like the moon. A humane pupil, missing from her eyes.

"What do you want, boy?" she said with slight harshness, turning to admire her shelves of cursed paraphernalia.

Gulping, clearing my throat I managed an introduction.

"I—I am John Sawyer, Miss. John Sawyer of the Sawyer Carpenters in Scotland."

"A Scotsman?"

I had clearly piqued her interest as she turned to face me again. I felt unease, spying that cradled in her hands she held a mouse, her thumb rotating gently caressing the creatures head. I pondered if the creature was as scared as I was.

"Y—yes."

Before I could say more, the ethereal voice of the hag continued, "Ahh, Scottish blood is very valuable these days, my child."

The hag began caressing my face too with her cracked curling nails and grey hands. I felt like the mouse.

"Those witches and practitioners of voodoo magic would pay handsomely for your blood. Watch your back, John Sawyer of the Sawyer Carpenters."

I felt threatened and backed into a corner. 12-year-old me knew this feeling. Holding a jagged rock in his shaky hands, tears streaming down his face, while adjacent from him stood an equally youthful wolf. Backed into a cave, with nothing but a stone wall against my back. I still remember so clearly, the gnarls of the wolf, its growls and its predator stalking movements, slowly creeping around my sides, creating an angle from which it could strike. Reliving that moment in the hag's hut brought a strong confidence, a fighting response out in me from deep within my subconscious.

"I can care for myself, hag. My father spoke of a witchblood here, amongst the plains of England. One that spoke to the skies and recited poems to the lakes. Do you know of such a witch blooded creature?"

The hag turned from me again muttering to herself. I questioned if she was trying to remind herself of the witch I spoke of, or if she was trying to curse me.

"John Sawyer. I believe the witch you seek is named Cassandra Boyle. Nasty bit of work she is. She appears to people in their darkest hour. I know nothing else of her, Scotsman."

"Cassandra Boyle. Do not lie to me, woman! I have travelled days and nights to be here. I am far from home and you of all people shall know what the wildlands will try to do with you."

17

"I am well aware, boy. Leave. I believe Mr Brickenden will be coming around again shortly. You have met him, haven't you?"

I left the hag laughing and I ran from the stick and stone hut to find Yen resting by a tree. The moon still centred the night sky, the stars still bright, painting the darkness with light. I knew Mr Brickenden, or the creature he was now, would be back soon.

"Yen, we must leave the East Woods. Now."

War is when you see the true colours of mankind. The clash of iron and cries of men, as blood spills on a battlefield, is when the real souls of people can be seen. It was the height of the civil war; the green vegetation hadn't been spotted in weeks. Fire and smoke ate away at the environment. Piles of bodies burned, the stench cleared villages and drew crows from afar. I remember as a boy, Father sent me out to make some more coin for the family. He always had the idea that one day, we would all earn enough to buy a way out of the damned country. To the land across the ocean, where the delicate scent of freshly baked bread woke up the villagers. The land where the kings and noblemen were warm hearted, and almost forced the land to flourish and thrive. Where people knew not the shade of their neighbours' blood. The dream was farfetched, but in a country where a witch blooded woman can conjure storms and influence the tongues of flame in a bonfire, it certainly wasn't impossible. My role in achieving this dream, was to earn the coin to pay for wood, so my father could carve the runes and other wonders of carpentry. I remember, clear as day, running across an abandoned battlefield, just moments after the last man was struck down. I was taught to look for the soldiers with the red

18

eye painted on their shields and armour. These were men who were valuable to their commanding officers. The red eye represented the battalions of the Scots, said to protect those who drew blood in the name of the country. I knelt next to one of the aforementioned men, my knees sinking into the loose soil. To this day I'm unsure how a child of 12 could keep a steady hand whilst rummaging through the pockets of a dead man. My young lungs drew in heaps of air, air in which you could taste the iron. The pockets of soldiers and knights typically held small trinkets and enchanted items. Basic witchcraft and alchemy could craft such an item, and my heart would sink seeing the declining value on the market. I would do anything to please my father…

The wood was silent, yet my thoughts screamed. Thoughts of fear, of the Hag, of the beast that was Mr Brickenden, that I might never return home. All I could envision was my defensive guard tight as the jaws of the animal clamped on my arms, crimson blood spraying, painting his bristled fur. Both myself and the misunderstood farmer Yen, panted like a rogue dog chasing a rabbit. I could hear the heavy exhales and sharp inhales. Running, while trying to piece together the way back to the Burncorn Village, the way out of the East woods. My dry eyes veered a bit too far off the path, and an obscure figure of a beast could be seen. The size of a bear, yet slender and fast, it bounded on all fours in the treeline. I knew it could find us; we could never escape it whilst still in the presence of the woods. All the monster would have to do is smell the fear. The fear that was ingrained in every droplet of sweat that travelled from my brow.

"Yen, get us out of here!" I shouted to him.

There was no more reason to be quiet. Mr Brickenden had found us.

"I—I could've sworn it was this way. Only couple hundred more paces and we'll be out."

I sensed a doubt in the voice of Yen. Then the rustle of the movement beside us stopped and our party also halted.

"It's lost us," Yen stated.

"No. No it couldn't have. Beasts like that can smell prey miles off. It's flanking us."

I was never an animal expert, but I knew that beasts were deadly trackers. Father used to talk of how they lined up on the shoreline because they could smell people from nearby countries. Another feeling boiled inside me, not above the anxiety of death, nor above the anger at the Hag of the East woods whom I internally blamed for our current predicament. Up just above the tree line, a starling flew overhead, singing a familiar tune. Before I could rationally think, my legs had already made the decision to bolt in the opposite direction to our original 'way out'.

"Hey, where you going, foreigner?" Yen shouted after me.

"Hurry, you old goat," I responded.

The forceful words of encouragement ensured Yen would follow closely. This time, my eyes peeled on the starling that bounced across the night sky. And even chance couldn't have predicted, the euphoric sight that blessed my life. I collapsed onto the grass, in the clearing, free from the dark grasps of the treeline, and free from the jaws of Mr Brickenden. Yen lay next to me, he too teary eyed, and wheezing from the sprint. "Hey… not bad, John Sawyer."

The approval of a hard-working self-made farmer meant more to me than that of any royal or nobleman. Finally, I was out of the East woods. I had escaped the devilish schemes of the Hag who resided there. Survived an encounter with a beast so terrifying it had killed the man Mr Brickenden and took his body. And I had a name. The witch blood, Cassandra Boyle.

Chapter 3

Unlikely Friends and Devilish Foes

Days passed since my ventures in Burncorn. Last I saw the farm man Yen, I shook his hand placing a silver coin in his hand, as he placed a copper one in mine.

"Copper coin for ye. Blessed by that exorcist folk. Any room you stay in, place in the centre under the door. No ghosts or ghouls will be welcome."

I pushed the coin into the shirt pocket, before gently patting it, to assure myself it was there.

"Thank you, Yen. I now search for Cassandra Boyle. Further down the hole."

"Yeah, well I remember speaking to the Botsmans. When their kid went missin', they spoke to one of those people that can walk the astral plane. Makes findin' people a whole lotta easier."

"Do you know where I could find one of these people? These astral plane walkers?"

"I ain't too sure, but I know a lot of those weird, supernatural folk are in Freshwater. Exorcists and that."

I thanked Yen endlessly for his gratitude. Yen was a kind man. He had the life many veterans from the war dreamed of. Despite being broken, he wasn't haunted by the spectres of his slain enemies and he had enough coin to survive. The simple life. The wildlands did not ease up, its vicious winds and sinking ground. Every step I took felt as though my boot fell deep into the soil, like walking through quicksand. Rain battered the hood of my cloak; the harsh weather did not want me to find the witchblood. So many questions circled my head.

Father once said, "Witchbloods. Don't trust them. If the darkness has infected their kin with magic and their words with curses, they are not the people you want to sort with."

Never had I seen a witchblood before. The tales of their manipulative and dastardly behaviour only ever reached my father's ears who then spilt those words to me. Whilst I pondered such thoughts, I spied a light in the distance. My new destination was Freshwater Town. I had heard rumours of an astral walker who resided there. One who might be able to find the witchblood in question. However, Freshwater was a few moons trip and the light in the distance would serve as shelter from the night. I approached cautiously, like a deer to an open field, the sign of the Taproom read 'The Bats Wings'. Upon entering the establishment, I was greeted by a room of characters. Characters you would only ever see in the dark, for they ran from the light. I stood at the bar, next to a gent, wearing rags and a crusty aged hat that fell over his shoulder and hung down his back. His forearms scarred in lettered scars 'BCO'. I had spent limited time in Burncorn village, but I knew what those brands were.

"Burncorn Outcast..." I muttered.

"What do ye wan… bastard." The slurred words barely made it past his protruding front teeth.

"Your story. Why did you get thrown from Burncorn?"

He turned back to his drink and staring deep into the liquid in his tankard he began.

"Leaves were falling from the trees. They looked so pretty you know. Especially this one oak tree next to me house. They kinda just floated down and gently caressed the ground. Life wasn't as simple. My wife and I struggled to pay the taxes. Every time the collectors came around, holding their bloody boxes my heart was in my throat. She always looked at me with those eyes and that smile. Never did I doubt her, and I always knew life would be okay even if we lost the house and our possessions cause we had each other. One evening, I had to collect wood to feed the fire. I was no woodsman, the cuts weren't clean, each block jagged and splintered. Fire isn't bothered by what feeds it, ya know? I placed all the wood in a sack, piecing it like an impossible puzzle. Dragging it along the path carved in the grass was the last thing I remember. Next time I opened my eyes I was holding her; blood… blood staining her white gown. There was so much of it, all over my hands. I can still see it all now. My hand was gripping a blade in her side. I cried, I cried so much, seeing just… seeing the one you love, with life leaving them. And I just didn't know. What had I done? And then soldiers came, the thuggish kind with their swords and god damned armour. They dragged me from her like I was some kind of, kind of an animal. By the time I could actually see without tears in my eyes, I had this brand on my arm, and I was out here to be killed by the monsters."

Then the drunken man cried. Rubbing his eyes so hard, his fingers turned white and you could make out his eye sockets. "I'm sorry. There are people in Freshwater Town who might be able to let you speak with your…"

"I ain't talking to no magic blooded – I'm done with all this voodoo, occult and magic crap. All I need now is this tankard. I ain't gonna leave," he said, burying his face back in his tankard.

My room was no larger than a cupboard. Straw leaked from the sides of the bed, and the far side post creaked should you step too close. I knelt on the floor and gently slid the copper coin underneath the centre of the door. I had great faith in Yen and refused to believe that the coin did anything it wasn't supposed to. I laid on the thin mattress, the straw itching my back and let my mind wonder. Wonder of all I had witnessed since I left the comfort and safety of my home. I had never seen such beasts and horrors. Could I ever make it home again? I doubted, doubted that I would make it back without some sort of scarring from a tooth or blade and a curse hanging over my soul. Listening to the tales from the mouths of such broken characters whom I had encountered, I couldn't believe I was still unscathed. Men of such a tough and strong prowess that had become mere drunks stumbling from taproom to taproom, hoping that the earth would swallow them. My father was like them. The first memory of my father lies deep inside my head. I remember clumsily walking up a hill in a wood. With the curiosity of such a child, I led astray from the path becoming lost in all the identical trees and shrubs. So, I did what any child would do. I fell to my knees and tears streamed down my face while echo's shouting for him left my tongue. To my father, it was the voice of his scared, young child screaming for help. However, to other animals and beasts, it was the sound of prey. Down from the heavens soared a falcon, one on which fire blessed its feathers. It towered over any man, its talons breaking the treeline. Clear as day, I remember my father running from my right to tackle the bird. The battle they created is just a blur to me now. What I can remember, is my father and the falcon locked, exchanging fierce attacks in a fiery inferno. He wrestled the winged beast to the ground, and through its torso he spiked his farmers fork. Looking back on it as I lay on the bed of hay, I question what he would've told me to do in the presence of a beast like Mr Brickenden. Should I have leaped from the bushes from which I was hiding, wrapped my hands around the beast's throat, and proceed to tear his jaw open like a walnut from its shell? What kind of man was I, that in the slightest sign of danger I ran in terror? I was uncertain.

Some misunderstand the power of dreams. Dreams are raw subconscious energy. People in the marketplaces among the towns and villages that rain salt water sell bottled dreams to noblemen. A way out of the harsh reality in which they are imprisoned and a chance to be free. Most importantly, dreams are private. So why, in this deep slumber of mine, did I witness the starlin' from East Woods perched on a branch, staring into my eyes almost waiting for me to speak.

"You could say, your welcome?" the bird said, as it twitched its head.

"You… can speak?"

"Are you surprised? You've witnessed man become beast, flaming birds and evil hags. A speaking starlin' should come to no shock."

"You… you've looked around my head."

"Well, flying here isn't all that fun. I was becoming rather fatigued while I sat waiting for you to drift off into this sleep." I was confused at the idea that this bird had somehow made its way into my dreams, and even more so, I was angry that it welcomed itself to the memories deep in my mind.

"What are you doing here? I saw you in East Woods?"

"Yes, well I am no ordinary creature as you can see. I need your help. You seek a man who scours the astral plane are you not?"

"Yes... how did you—"

"There isn't time to explain. His name is Tirynn of Freshwater. You can't trust him."

The bird knew that the man I was looking for was from Freshwater town. He couldn't be lying, could he? I had to push further.

"Yet somehow, you expect me to place my trust in a speaking starlin?"

"I will become an asset to your journey, not a burden. I can help you find the witchblood you seek."

"How do you know of the witchblood?"

The bird fluttered its wings in an irritation before strongly responding, "Listen, there isn't time. I know of your mother. Find me."

My eyes crept open, the orange sun glowing through the window. A feeling of nausea infested in my stomach, the kind when anxiety builds up, and the sort when you've been under the influence of some sort of magic, or spell. Could the starlin be real? It could've been some young witch or child playing with my dreams, moulding them like clay. Or... it could be that the starlin is a member of this reality, that it knows the witch blood I need to find, and it... somehow it knows of my

27

mother. Droplets of rain and pellets of hail bombarded my route to Freshwater. And the water fed the grounds, the weeds and the vegetation breathed new life, life I had never before seen. Like waves the hills and mounds moved. The rising and falling, the hills moved effortlessly and with such ferocity. Trees were uprooted, their 100-year life brought to an abrupt end by the earth in which they were sustained for a century as it was torn from beneath them. Thunders clapped and lightning responded. Bolts thrown from the clouded skies lit the oceans of green alight. I knew danger was imminent, my heart pounded within my chest and to my ears, appeared louder than the thunder itself. I was moving swiftly and was no longer able to distinguish the difference between what was my perspiration and what was the cold water drops from the heavens. I ran close to the ground and every few paces I was forced to take a knee from the ever-moving tide like the swaths of earth were removed from beneath me. Now, tears also blessed my face. I curled up on the waves of the wildlands, tears streaming from my eyes as I shut them so tight, nothing could be seen but darkness and occasionally red spots. The thunder echoed in my mind; the constant booming followed by the violent flashes of lightning. Fear controlled my breathing, hyperventilation followed by the moans and cries of the need to return home. I tried to imagine home, the Scottish Highlands, the mountains and rivers that ran through them. Then boom goes the thunder, like a parent taking a child's toy, I am slapped back into the reality that I am curled up in the middle of the moors of England. The moors that are alive and well aware that I am not welcome. Hours pass, and slowly the ground begins to solidify and freeze back to the norm. The thunder had had its fun and left taking its siblings of lightning and rain with it. The clouds from the sky began to dissipate, revealing the layers of endless stars in the clear night sky. I rolled to lay on my back. Unbeknown to me my breathing halted, becoming the gentle inhale and exhale I was once aware of. All my senses are dulled, except for my sight which is in a state of awe and sheer amazement. Staring up at the stars, all huddled around the moon the lunar rays shining through my tear jerked eyes. And for the first time in my life, miles away from home I finally fell in love. Not with an entity but with a feeling. The feeling of true peace, looking up at the stars. The calm… after the storm.

Chapter 4

The Gate to Freshwater

Wondering through the night had taken its toll. Despite the peace I had met that night, I felt nothing but a dreaded sense unease as I approached the gates to Freshwater town. Unlike Burncorn, this town had more etiquette. A large wall built from logs and the labour of many circled the town, all residents based on the inside. Two watchmen stood watch at the gates of the town, and I was sure they would have questions as to why a Scottish man walks among them?

"H—hello, I am er, John Sawyer. I was informed you have an astral walker here. I need to talk with him."

The unease in my voice was probably not a comforting tone to fall upon the ears of these men.

"Ah. Right then. You, a trader?" one of them said.

He didn't sound much like a knight. Knights were of noble heritage. Honourable and respectful warriors. Most knights were blessed by the light from the sun upon their first battle. Tales from the armies of darkness stated that the Knights of King Ichilla were 'unkillable'.

"Trader? No, no see. I'm just here on business that is all."

"An' you expect us to let you into our town? Nah, mate; what if your vampiric like that other girl we let in here?"

"Vampiric? I promise you; I've never encountered a vampiric being before, let alone a lass. I promise you have nothing to fear."

The two conversed before turning back to me, the one on the left stumbled downhill and checked my strap bag for weapons.

"Tell you what, Scotsman. We let you in, but you leave right after your done with your 'business'."

I thanked the two knights before entering the town. Buildings erected from stone and concrete created a maze on the inside of the great walls. I wandered the columns of stone before coming to a town centre, an open area. The town was named freshwater because it was built upon the first fresh water source discovered among the wildlands of England, or so it was told. The town sold its water and made its coin, enough to become proud and well off. Exorcists were common in these parts. They tended to travel from afar, much like myself, to purchase freshwater which could then be blessed and used to expel demonic creatures and ghosts. Exorcists had a very recognisable guise, one of a black cloak and hood, with bottles, vials and silver discretely hidden on their person. Many people in England and even Scotland feared the exorcists. Rumours that they were even more skilled than knights, spiked fear and worry in the hearts of many. There was a tale once of an exorcist who lived long, and the job became his life. He knew how to expel almost any being of darkness. He became great. However, the enemy of time cannot be beaten, as his hair slowly shrivelled and turned a wolf grey. His frame became battle-hardened, yet frail and delicate. The exorcist had a sister, a beautiful woman. Some say her eyes always reflected the sun, even when it rested.

Many men of the town asked for her hand in marriage, all wishing to place a ring upon her gentle hand. However, one man wanted her more than any. His love for her ached at his soul and love is a powerful motivator, one that can force a person to do horrible things. Jealous that he wasn't the man of her dreams, he bought a powerful venom. A venom from the fangs of a giant cave dwelling serpent, corrosive enough to burn through the scales of a dragon. He lured the young woman in and used the chemical to deform her face certain that if he couldn't have her, then he would make sure no other man could. Now, even though her brother, the exorcist, was an aged man, he was still deadly. Using his skills and abilities, he found a horrible spirit. The spirit was impulsive, obsessive, and manipulative. The exorcist forced the spirit down the man's evil gullet, deep inside till it reached his soul. He then recited holy words burning the man's inside, like an ember touching timber, the evil man erupted burnt from the inside out. Exorcists, priests, alchemists, and experts on people who are affected by vampirism or lycanthropy all resided in the stone weathered homes of Freshwater. The village of Freshwater, in my eyes, was deceptively calm and peaceful. However, if one had wondered the plains long enough, they would see the village as a scar on the country, a broken village, and a mere shadow of what it could have become. Edging my way through the inhabitants of the town, my shoulders brushing with people who too had a history dealing with the dangers of this cursed country, my foreign eyes scanned for a sign I was heading towards the astral walker. Abruptly after this seemingly endless wondering, I was gifted with such a sign. A small room, on the corner of a much larger church. Could this really be the home to one of 'the most talented astral walkers in England'? Like a fawn entering a dark wood, I stumbled into the room. From the ceiling hung spiders' silk, the small bones, and skulls of less fortunate woodland creatures. In this room, predator and prey alike hung in the same manner, their pelts covering the walls as the dim glow of an orange candle flickered against them. Then, like an unexpected punch to the gut, I knew that life was going to become much harder. The centre of the room was cluttered, furniture thrown from corner to corner, blood stained the blankets on the floor, and a blade protruded from the north wall.

"Aye, they took him, didn't they?" an aged voice spoke just behind my ear.

I pivoted around to face the fellow who spoke with an experienced grizzled voice.

"Who are you? Tirynn?" I queried.

The figure stepped into the light of the centre of the room, revealing a child.

"Tirynn? No, no. Names, William Thorn. If you do see that bastard, feel free to sock him from me."

Confusion flooded my mind yet again, a reoccurring phenomenon since I arrived in England. A child speaking with the voice of an elder? Sadly, not a word he said found its way to my ears.

"Sorry, what?" I said again, before the child, William, moped to the dagger in the wall, using his skinny arms to begin wriggling it from its resting place.

"I told ya. Names, William Thorn. Tirynn? He's an ass."

Fortunately, William realised why my cloud of confusion was taking time to dissipate.

"Ah, right, the appearance can be off putting, I getcha. Well it wasn't my choice. Even though yer a Scotsman I'm sure your aware with curses and possession and such?"

I nodded hastily. I had been informed of the danger of curses before I left home. I was always told of how curses were the devils whispers in your ear. Only those whose souls were as evil as the fabric of hell itself could perform such curses. I had never intended to meet such a person on my travels. William took a few seconds of silence to analyse the knife. He brought the blade close to his eyes, before rotating it slowly looking at the broad side, and the point itself.

"Ah, lucky for you, son, I know where he is. He's been taken by those Cult of Jordinn folk."

"Why would they want him?" My fast response came across as being defensive.

"I don't know, probably want him killed who knows, boy, what do you expect me to know? Tirynn has screwed a lotta people over in his time… lads an idiot. Come on then, s'pose we should go get him…"

William and I left the safety of the town of freshwater, and yet again my boots tasted the fresh soil of the wildlands. My sense of anxiety was calmed as I had a guide, but one can never be too calm on the plains.

"So, what brings you here, foreigner?" he asked.

He led a few paces and sniffed the wind like a dog. It was fascinating.

"I… I seek a woman…"

"Ahh, hoping to get lucky, are ya? I know a gent's bar in town."

"No, no, not like that… She's witchblood."

34

"Oh. Well yer going to need a blade and some blessings my friend. Witchbloods panic when ya corner them. They freak out. Start trying to get hell spawns to bite yer head off ha-ha."

The way William spoke of witchbloods with such confidence and familiarity was intriguing. Could that be why he's in the body of a child? I had never thought I would have to fight anyone. The idea of entering in a battle of magic, curses, and summons with a witchblood made my heart race. William's voice was no longer coherent however, ever present in my ears was the thudding rhythmic beats of my heart. I felt my legs become weak and every mount in the soil became a challenge to step over. I had always heard tales of humans dying to witchbloods, vampires and lycanthropic beings alike. I couldn't battle them; I was no knight or exorcist or mage. Suddenly I became very aware of the weight of my head and limbs. I fell to my knees, denting the wet grass, my irregular breathing becoming apparent to William who stopped trundling along and turned to look at me.

"Ah, come on, foreigner. We are almost there."

Then he turned and continued pacing onwards. The lack of sensitivity or care in his voice told me the sort of treatment I was in for with this guide. The thoughts planted by William of our imminent arrival, was not what made me get to my feet again. It was simply the idea that if a child could wander the plains without fear, then I could too. And stumbling over another hill or two, we arrived at the tomb, where the Cult of Jordinn practiced their dark arts, and where we would hopefully find the astral walker Tirynn.

Chapter 5

The Tomb of the Cult of Jordinn

The Cult of Jordinn were a unique group of people. Hundreds of years they would waste away locked in a tomb only leaving to find new blood to sacrifice to their elder gods. Most villages believed them to be nothing but folk lore, simply tales around a campfire. I believed similarly, until I was confronted by the entrance to their sacred tomb. The structure was a rounded hollow, with runes and carvings around the surrounding stone. From the cracks and fractures in the wall's vines spewed, like snakes slithering down and tainting the floor in vegetation. However, upon entering the tomb another of my senses came under attack. A stench of rotting corpse filled my nostrils, a stench I was quick to exhale covering my mouth with the sleeve of my garment.

"What is that? Smells like the war. Like a battlefield."

"Aye, ain't you a perceptive one? Nah, boy, that smells from the mix of blood an' limestone. Gotta remember, this place ain't had new air in decades," William said, as he crept further into the doorway, before halting gazing down into the dark depths of a staircase.

The staircase itself was like its own entity that wanted us dead, a thick blanket of moss made the stone underneath barely visible, and each step I went down I was left unsure if my next would force me to tumble down to the bottom. The stairs seemed to have less of an effect on William who bounded down them as if they held no sort of threat to him. In the little time I had known him, the realisation dawned on me that the man had little sense of fear. Despite being trapped in a child's body, he appeared completely fearless. Such a man reminded me of my father, a man who seemed unphased by the threatening nature of the world. As each step of my boots echoed through the stairways, I posed a question to William.

"Do you have any sense of fear at all, Thorn?"

"Fear? Of what? What is there to fear? Worse case, ya die. An' death? Ah deaths coming for all of us anyway. I knew a gent once, who actually spoke to death an' said he was a nice guy."

"But…"

"Eh… John was it? Listen you're missing the point. How do you know we ain't just a witch familiar? That we aren't just God's dream and as soon as the big man wakes, we go poof? If nothing is real, what do we have to fear?"

"Something is real, otherwise there would be nothing to conjure this illusion of life you seem convinced of?"

My response forced a slight grin in the corner of William Thorn's mouth before he responded.

"If we are in God's dream, how do we know of his existence? How can we be sure of anything? It's an all or nothin' scenario. An' you gotta make a choice. Is everything real? Or is nothing real? Do you have a choice at all? Or is choice just an illusion too?"

Reaching the bottom of the steps concluded our journey into the depths of the tomb, yet the existential thoughts planted in my mind by William still were very much alive. The darkness was thick and seemed to emit a sense of danger.

A sense that repulsed the instinctive nature to 'stay alive' provided by the human mind. Thorn and I were faced with a corridor of darkness, which we carefully advanced through, and in doing so began to hear the rhythmic chants echoing from further down.

"The cultists?" I questioned.

"Hmph… Bastards can pray all they want, I won't stop them, so long as they give me Tirynn. That pig…"

I was yet to understand why Tirynn, the Astral Walker, had a reputation similar to that of a ghoul or phantom. An irritation or parasite had a cleaner conscience. Joining the sound of the chants, was the clanging of metal chains and the sharp chyme of a key being forced into a rusted lock. To the surprise of both myself and William, the further we travelled along the seemingly endless corridor, the darkness began to clear. William instructed me to halt. I knelt beside him and peered over his shoulder, into a clearing. Inhabiting the clearing, a group of people in white cloaks, their faces masked. The masks they donned left a permanent scar in my mind, for it appears they had skinned the face of pigs, cows, and sheep and took them for their own.

"Sick fuckers, eh? Apparently, they do it to keep them 'clean'."

William's insight to the Cult of Jordinn proved that he was a reliable ally. I sat back and leant against the stone wall. My breathing began to slip away from me, and my hands became erratic. My mind slowly filled with thoughts, first of my journey here, then of events that hadn't occurred. What if the cultists found us and skinned us to? Could they really summon gods? Questions abruptly appeared in my head and refused to leave. I shut my eyes tight and begged for it all to go away. I felt a pat on my knee, upon opening my eyes I saw William, but his words didn't reach my ears, as if my mind refused to hear anything he had to say. Slowly the sound of chanting become apparent again, followed by the words,

"Come on, dumbass, get a hold of yourself."

He then pointed over to a cell just across the room, where a man sat, blonde long hair over his bloodied face which had spilt down his front becoming a brown stain on his rags.

"That, John, is Tirynn the astral walker."

Under the cover of darkness, we waited patiently. The cultists had begun to gather around an open fire chanting in a language I had never heard and couldn't begin to interpret. Like the sharp howl of a lycanthropic being, their words became less and less human. The words communicated with the flame, which too began to dance and split in ways no natural embers could. The orange tongues fluctuated and, in the rhythm of the chants, began to spit new colours of emerald. While the cultists had become besotted with their green fire, William bolted for the cell door, and I was quick to follow. Drawing his knife, William Thorn began to jam it in the keyhole, wriggling it. The snap of metal from within the locks, caused a few of the cultists nearby to realise our presence. They continued to speak in unknown tongues, while pointing at me and William.

"Ah shit." He moaned, dropping his knife from the lock to the mossy rock floor.

The inside of the cell was damp. Hay bales acted both as warmth, food, and a bed to whoever was unlucky enough to be trapped inside. The man who William claimed to be

Tirynn, still hadn't moved from his position since our abrupt and untimely arrival. The cultists seemed to have little interest in us. I suppose we didn't pose much of a threat to them. It's not as if we were exorcists or knights from King Ichilla's royal guard. We weren't even soldiers or farmers. To the untrained eye we appeared to be a weary, frightened traveller and a young foul-mouthed boy. However, I knew William was clever. Despite his appearance of a nine-year-old boy, I was sure he had years of experience dealing with, not only the occult but with other demons and beasts that lurked the wildlands.

"Are you, Tirynn? Hello?" I whispered, edging close to him, and nudging his leg. "My name's, John Sawyer... I need your help."

"Does it look... like we are in any position to be making decisions now?" his deep grisly voice came forth from his mouth, each vowel and syllable enunciated like a scholar from a priest or mage in the high cities within the wildlands.

As he spoke, more blood trickled from his mouth, revealing his stained teeth and only half a tongue remaining within his jaw.

"Err... No I guess not... sorry, sir," I muttered back, before distancing myself from him on the other side of the cell.

I never wanted to be a burden, nor an irritation. I knew that Astral Walking was a limited profession in the wildlands, and if I were to find the witchblood Casandra Boyle, I would need one to point me in the right direction. I cast myself back to when I was a young boy, and my father and I trekked for a couple moons to get to the nearest village. The village was said to have a talented astral walker. See, I complained to father about where my mother was a lot. He always used to shake his head, the vain slowly pushing from his forehead, before muttering some nonsense about his next building project. He would then force me out the house to hunt for food, and it was at that point I knew that the question would find no answer with him, and I should just try to forget about it and focus on the more important things such as survival.

Is this redemption? Is this a light I see before my eyes? The thoughts weighed heavy in my dazed mind. The light was dim, but in the darkness it was brighter than the north star. This was a chance for change, a way out from the deep abyss from which I was born and raised. I was shown a door, a way out from the pain and anguish that stained my soul for many moons. This was the door to salvation, the chance for a new start, a fresh start. The darkness cradled me, like a mother would her infant. It recognised me, and likewise I knew it. I knew it all too well. I always ran from it; at first, I was afraid. But soon, I stopped running. I fell into its welcoming arms, and the shadows gripped my mind and refused to let me go. This light, this way out was foreign and different. I had learned the darkness, and the light frightened me even more. I stepped into the light and its rays bathed my skin. I placed every faith in the dim light that stood alone in the dark abyss. The light that had found its way to me. My little light.

I jolted awake, as if a heard a familiar whisper behind my ear. A cold sweat fell from my head, opposite me the two people I had now become cell mates with conspired.

"So, I'll grab that ol' bastard and tear his head off," William grunted to Tirynn who still wore the face of a widower.

I kept quiet. Despite perhaps giving the impression that I would be willing to follow these men into battle, or the misconception that us scots were born to be violent and merciless, there was a deep sense of anxiety around combat, one which I refused and was rather unwilling to explore. Before I could question their plans or give my own input on strategy, William waltz to the bars of the cell, his demeanour changing from a nihilistic old man in a child's body, to a confident and suave young man.

"Excuse me, lads, I'm still a kid, ya know… Gotta tell me parents where I am and that."

Like a fisherman he began to work his irresistible charm, dragging in cultists who watched the cell like hawks. And so, I watched as a battle of mental and psychological warfare raged. No sword was drawn, or armour pierced. No clanging of metal or bashing of shields. I watched as the purest form of combat took place, as one mind prevailed over another. Through his words and actions William constricted his prey, wrapping around it and squeezing. I could see how the odds of survival for the man who approached the cell became very slim as William continued to select and choose particular words and sentences to draw the man in and position him mentally and physically at the most disadvantaged place possible. In a short and quick motion, William Thorn disarmed the man from the Cult of Jordinn, pulling out a dagger from his belt one which would only be seen on display, a piece not meant for war for its brittle nature and antique design. The flaws in this piece of weaponry did not phase William, for his intended use was to draw blood. He didn't care if the blade struggled to break the skin of his foe, for he would force the blade, twisting and turning it until it did. He didn't care if the blade snapped in the throat of his enemy, for he would proceed to use the hilt to cave another man's skull. Despite the appearance of a child, Williams nature was one of violence and aggression. The door to the cell swung open, William running to tackle another cultist member. By now, many had heard the clang and screech of the cell door open, and the patter of footsteps down the moss stairs were constant like rain. Tirynn ran past me, shoving me out the way as he went to join the fight. And yet again I found myself frozen, unable to act. My eyes were compulsorily drawn to the man on the floor, wearing a pigskin mask, as blood seeped from his throat painting the floor in a crimson that could only be found inside the bloodstream of a human. I felt my breathing become rigid and unpredictable. A power from inside me, the nature of the mind to survive erupted, and my legs began to move. Everything around me become nothing but a blur of red splashes and the vague outlines of war, as I rushed through the crowd of people. Visually, I was impaired at this moment in time, however my ears were very much awake. I heard every slash. I heard every grunt and thud as punches were thrown and blades were thrusted. I heard the screams of men as they realised their death was imminent. Some appeared to be confused, feeling no sense of pain, yet they leaked blood at a fatal rate. And lastly, I heard the silent yet very real sound as their souls were collected by death as it took them to the next life. Panicked I rushed up the steps, clambering before slipping onto all fours. This wouldn't stop me, as I persisted and with the aid of all four limbs the exit of the tomb was in sight. And the light of a breaking dawn blessed my being again.

Leaning against a nearby tree I squeezed my eyes shut. My father had always told me what war was like. I know in my youth I had aspirations of knighthood, however all I envisioned was the shiny medals, the equally shiny armour, and the banquets so big, that you could devour all the food in a city. I had never seen a life be taken before. And yet, prior to this I recently witnessed a bloodbath, as men who I considered to be ally's mercilessly slaughtered other men. My morals have always been near enough angelic. I had a natural sense of right and wrong, good, and bad, since I was a boy. I knew what it meant to be good. Staying within the light, and not straying from the path into one of darkness and doom was something I had managed to accomplish till now. And despite not taking part in the massacre at the Tomb of the Cult of Jordinn, my conscience felt tainted. I felt a part of me separate and drift off, left forever to wonder that tomb. I felt that when I die, my ghost will be forced back to the tomb as a being of higher consciousness forces me to gaze upon my sins. I battled with the good and bad in my mind, the light and darkness. Did I do wrong? The cultists were bad people? But they were still people, nevertheless. And I didn't stop the murder, instead I ran like a coward, running from the battle, my fears and anxiety plucking me from the tomb and out where I could finally breathe, and my heart could finally slow down. I had become very aware of my heartbeat, feeling every beat shake my body, hearing each pump. Soon it was all I could hear, as the noise of the gentle breeze and the songs of birds drowned out. Then the ever-growing sound of screams and the flashes of red presented themselves through my closed eyes before, Williams voice uttered.

"Oi, where were you during that?"

William stumbled from the tomb. His clothes stained a light red, and his face had a few flicks of blood placed up the centre.

"I… I."

"I'll tell you where he was… he ran… he ain't ever seen blood before… have ya, Scotsman?"

I had no idea what character trait it was that Tirynn possessed but his condescending tone was definitely one that I despised. The two of them treated death carelessly, like it was no different from bathing, or changing your clothes. I made a mental note never to become like them. Once my breathing become somewhat tangible, I made a comment to Tirynn and William, who were now clasping their blades in their shirts, wiping the blood off them revealing a pristine, metallic blade.

"Death is not something I treat lightly."

But before I had the chance to speak further, he spoke,

"No, Scotsman. Death is just a passage to a different life. I'm sure they will find their way back here if they be determined enough. Don't assume that you hold a moral high ground foreigner. They were monsters. We are all monsters."

Clumps of mud gathered on the underside of my boots, every twenty or so paces I had to stop and use a stick to scrape it, if I wanted to keep walking that is. I strayed back from the others. I felt a certain unease around them and struggled to place what it was. I felt as if I was in the wrong place. My quest to simply arrive in England to deliver a rune, had become such a commotion. One that involved a wooded area, lycanthropic beings, void walkers, and cultists.

Chapter 6

Confession of Nightmares

Re-entering the town of Freshwater, we arrived as heroes. The lunatic William was soaked in the applause and gifts from others. It was as if people had convinced themselves that he was a God like character, sent to earth to bring Tirynn back home. While the gifts were being given and compliments were being thrown, the corner of my eye spied the vague shape of a man who darted into the deep dark of a valley between two buildings. I stopped; anxiety began to build. I felt a certain pull towards the valley, one that bothered me and deterred me, yet it felt so recognisable. Before I could deconstruct the mass of feeling that came over me enough to have rational thought, my body began to act on its own, led by the instinctual feelings pumped by my heart. The darkness of the alley was cold, and it was almost as if it was its own separate place in freshwater. The stone on the ground hadn't seen the light of the sun in decades, meaning the vibrant yellowish tint remained strong, unlike the faded stone around the rest of the village. Eyesight became nothing but myth in this place. My hands became outstretched in front of me, and I became very conscious of each step, patiently waiting for the awkward moment of hitting a wall or turning and running back to the light. Eyesight wasn't gifted in this place however hearing became as strong as that of a bat. The slight but noticeable ruffles of movement became further apparent the more I moved into the dark.

"You may as well take a seat then," a mumbled voice emitted.

Such a thing would usually spike fear, however, the familiarity of the voice echoed in my head. Those simple words I heard played over and over. It was a voice I was almost certain I had never heard before, yet behind the voice was a feeling, a mind, a consciousness that resonated with me.

I cautiously outreached my hands as I began to feel for the wall and lower myself to sit. I had no idea where the voice was, nor did I care. It was present in that moment with me, and despite being fearful, it was not fear of a threat.

"Speak... you know why you're here. You feel it. You are aware of it in your mind. Its present there, and although you may not see it, taste it, or hear it. It's still very real to you isn't it?"

"I... I've been having strange dreams and thoughts. I'm scared of what my mind is. I didn't want to admit it to myself. I didn't want it to become real."

"Explain your thoughts and dreams."

"I... I see myself fall into an abyss, into a darkness. I can see all I used to know, and love surrounded in fear, emitting it, like its pulsing. With each pulse, I feel the weight of it. Not because I'm afraid of giving up and letting go. I'm afraid of still standing. Deathly afraid of living day to day with nothing but the feeling of emptiness and being haunted. The echoes and whispers of darkness flowing through me with no escape. No sign of redemption or hope. I see myself trapped within a cage that I built. A constant fog that won't clear. An endless cycle of fear generated by a life in which I'm forced to live. By seeing what I feel a connection with turn from me. Seeing all I know leave; all I know change and adapt. To become disfigured to despise me. To become what I hate, to break me so even I begin to doubt, and self loathe. My mind begins to turn on itself, to bombard my fragile consciousness with questions and doubt. I feel interrogated by my own thoughts. My nightmares harrow me with these feelings and visions. Then I awake and think, *Has the nightmare even ended?* I awake to a reality filled with curses and beings so monstrous. A place where the rules and laws of life bend and mould to break you."

"Ah, yes, I do understand… but these are only surface thoughts, Scotsman. You must go deeper into discovering yourself."

"Deeper? I can't. If I go deeper, I fear I will never return from the nightmares. I can already feel them beckoning. They deceive me with the false hopes and images that I recognise. They show me what I want to see. They lie to me, and only when I wake am I plagued with feelings and thoughts. Fear begins to course through me the instant I awake to this reality. Fear is then accompanied by anger. I feel it swelling. Anger that these nightmares would disguise themselves as sympathetic and pleasant dreams, showing me everything I wish for. They show me the life I want and the life I could have before stripping it from me and forcing me awake in this reality where nothing exists, but the pain buried deep in my being."

"These nightmares… they define who you are. They belong to you for a reason… go to the cave of winters on the mountains of Terragoth. There you will find more answers of your nightmares. The next step on your journey."

Tirynn sat in his room, seemingly unphased by the destructive nature of the surroundings. All his belongings thrown askew, they held no sentimental value, most of them being vials of blood, or animal skulls and pelts. William leant in the doorway, and refused to move to grant me entry, meaning I had to squeeze past him, brushing close enough to smell liquor on his breath.

"Can I help you?" the astral walker said, as I stood adjacent.

"I came to find you. I was told you could help me find Cassandra Boyle, the witchblood?"

He rolled his eyes before giving a response with lacking enthusiasm. "And why would I do that?"

I was left in silence. I couldn't issue a threat; I posed no danger. Nor did I have anything to offer him in exchange. As these thoughts pondered in my mind, William piped up from behind me. He stumbled past me, his weight far too far forward over his toes. Tirynn slouched on his chair, a grin on his face as he observed the uncertain movements of William who proceeded to crush Tirynn's bony fingers under the butt of his knife.

"Listen, you bastard. We helped you once. I've heard the tales myself. Tirynn, the deceiver. Tirynn, the liar. Tirynn, the thief."

While William Thorn was delivering these lines, Tirynn let loose a few quiet whimpers, as he adjusted his body positioning in an attempt to relieve pressure from his broken hand.

"I don't like you anymore than I like those rats and the fleas they carry. We helped you out. We had a good time during the Massacre at the Tomb. Now be a good boy. Help him, then you help me."

"Y—yes it appears you have a problem, don't you?" Tirynn murmured from his still closed lips, gesturing to the childlike appearance of William with the hand that was still free.

William didn't take this comment lightly, as he proceeded to spin the knife around before driving it through the palm of Tirynn who abruptly let out a squeal.

Sweating, and shaky he said, "Heh... okay, child I will help your man friend."

The sight of blood which began leaking from his hand sparked the memories that plagued my mind from the tomb, however these were memories I chose not to engage at this moment in time. I had to deal with this and find the witchblood. Then I could leave this place. Tirynn stood from his chair, and staggered across the room, sneering at me as he passed, while crushing the bones that were scattered across the floor under his shoe. He held his impaled hand delicately as he moved to an attaching room, which was small enough to fit a small elf. The sort we would've stored blacksmithing items in at home. It housed a rather large velvet cushion, which Tirynn sat on and began to breathe heavily. I looked upon him in awe and confusion. He breathed like I did at the tomb, and when the storm was raging as I was travelling to Freshwater. But his was controlled, and unlike mine his wasn't in anxiety. It was for a purpose. His consciousness was ripped from his body and was thrown deep into the astral plane, far from the layers of reality we resided. While he was there his body was just that. Flesh, blood, and bone with no animation. Williams hand was subtly shaking, blood dripping from the dagger which he had previously removed from the hand of the astral walker. I reacted pre-emptively and moved fast to grab William, who in turn tried to enact his plan to butcher the empty body of Tirynn.

"No Thorn!"

"Do you have any idea what this animal has done to people? The people he's killed, the lives he's ruined?"

"I need him. Once he tells me what I must know, do with him what you will."

"No, no, John. You seem to have a conscience of gold but here, here is where you're wrong."

It wasn't so much the accusation that left the mouth of William that set off an immense rage that I had supressed unknowingly for years, but it was something deeper than that. Something I did not wish to uncover or explore at this moment in time.

"I'm wrong? I'm wrong for what? Because I disagree with you spilling this man's blood! Because I am a better man than to become the beckoner of death itself! I am here in this forsaken and damn cursed place for one reason. And if this man can help me then by god I will prevent his death till my dying breath. Don't you, 'William Thorn', try to stop me… please…"

The eyes of Tirynn flickered open, as if from a deep slumber which of course he was not. Scouring the planes of the Astral seemed too farfetched for me, I struggled to grasp the idea and because of that my mind rejected the concept. But if he could offer me a clue to the whereabouts of Cassandra Boyle then I would cooperate. As if his skills weren't only in astral walking, Tirynn seemed to be able to sense the tension in the room. It was almost as if the words spoken still remained in the room for him to listen to.

"You, gents, okay?" he enquired in the voice of a drowsy sleepless man.

"… Yeah… fine."

The words refused to leave William's lips, making them distort into a senseless grunt before he left the room.

"What did you find?"

"Eh, I searched for the witchblood you seek. It's in despair I tell you… she's dead."

Night graced the land with its presence yet again, the days becoming unbearably short. A deceptive silence befell the plains, only to be interrupted with a glancing breeze which disrupted the stillness of each needle of grass and branch. Even the noises of such creatures that haunted the land were not to be heard, only felt. I lay on a bed of straw, forgetting the last time I blinked. My dry eyes remain glued to the ceiling, almost the exact way they were when Tirynn told me those fateful words: 'She's dead.' How could she be dead? The one woman I travelled all these moons to see. I searched my mind, scouring my limited knowledge of how I could change the course of this decaying journey. I remember being told about death and its implications when I was a boy. It is believed that witchbloods are banished from the land of the dead. They conjure and contort their lives with magic. Their lives and souls are turned and twisted into a dark and damaged mirage of what it means to be human. Their being becomes so decayed and broken, death refuses them. Now that begs the question, what happens to witchbloods when they die? I had little idea. My expertise did not lie in these realms, nor did I know anyone who could aid me in finding out. As these thoughts bounced around the caverns of my head, flashes and shards of images etched into my mind. The visions of the snow-covered mountains of Terragoth. There lies the Cave of Winters, the one I was told to visit by the mysterious figure who spoke to me. I was unsure of what lies there, whether it be danger, riches or simply the echoes of an empty cave. But I did know that the nightmares that visited me relentlessly, the ones that carved memories of horror, the ones that I tried to supress with all my being... all could be explained at Terragoth.

Chapter 7

The Path to Terragoth

The instant night diminished, I left Freshwater. After my brief dispute with William, I did not feel compelled to wish him farewell. I appreciated all his efforts to aid my cause, but I could see he was a damaged man. One who could only find peace in vengeance, which could not be found on the path I was on. I left for the mountain region of Terragoth. The journey was some mere couple days, which didn't bother me for I had travelled much further before. What did concern me, was how the journey seemed too simple. The mountains were visible in the horizon, the tips of the mountains kissing the orange glow of dawn. I had heard very few tales of Terragoth. I had heard rumours of how the mountain feels your steps, and how travellers are but fleas on the back of a dog to it. The mountains can react and project images and illusions to toy with you, while the bitter cold brings out shivers, and the snow begins to gather on your boots. Each step becomes heavier, and each of your limbs begin to slow down, until your body becomes nothing but a statue of ice. Despite hearing these rumours, I refused to engage in the fear that accompanied them. While I was still walking the hills and grassy fields, I had little to worry of snow and ice. Thinking of survival reminded me of my time as a youth, under the tuition of my father. The Scottish Highlands were kind and would carry the echoes and rhythms of songs from afar. Despite this, the natural cold could still be threatening to mere mortals like us. I remember being up at a peak, so high the clouds passed around us like ghosts, and the stars were in arms reach. My father held a small candle, alight with a flame that grew dim and flickered with each passing moment, as the harsh cold battered its opposition. My father then did something I did not expect and to this day, remain unaware of how he learnt such a technique. He brought the flame close to his lips and spoke to it. He recited a poem, one which he claimed was spoken during the very first moons to force the sun into being. Once he had spoken to the flame, it flickered like a dance, and it was a strong ember that sat elegantly on the wick. The candle was lit for nine days after. My knowledge of that moment was limited, and I tried to recall the correct sequence of words to keep my flame alight, to bring me warmth and a glow so I could get to the cave unharmed. The grass wore thin, and pimples of rock became prominent on the land. The weather deteriorated, as the cold found its way to me. Engulfing bitter winds swirled around gnawing at my ears and leaking my eyes. Nearby I spied a thin wooded area. *If the trees could provide me cover from the harsh winds, I might yet live to see the Mountains of Terragoth,* I thought. I darted to the wood line, which to my surprise housed no life I could see, bar the odd woodlouse and maggot feasting on the rotting bark fallen from the trees of old. I perched against a tree looking out among the open fields. I saw a spectre, one carrying a bucket soaked in crimson, and despite the destructive winds seemed to move effortlessly across the wildlands.

"The smith father," I muttered, recalling the tale Yen first told me.

A sense of awe came over me, watching the spectre flow over the grounds. It was beautiful.

"He's a sad man. Best not interrupt him."

At this point, voices appearing from apparently nowhere no longer surprised me. Instead I scanned for the source of the voice. I turned and saw a pale man, far too pale to be living, his cold thin body chained to the base of a tree.

"I wouldn't dare," I said before turning back to become enthralled further by the ghost of the smith father.

"I heard he won't stop until his son returns to the land of the living... poor bastard doesn't understand he will be waiting a while."

"And you? Are you dead?"

"What gave it a way?" he said, swiftly followed by a chuckle.

"The chains, this malnourished body, or the fact I have no blood?"

"All of those I suppose... how did you end up here?"

I took opportunities like this to try and learn as much as possible. If I were to survive this venture and survive unscathed, I had to make sure I didn't end up like this gentleman.

"Ah!" the man said, while licking his lips, moistening them with a layer of saliva which proceeded to drip down his chin as he babbled. "What you're lookin at here, young fella, is a lifetime of mistakes. Each sin carved into a link in this chain. Now I'm forever bound to this forsaken wood! Couldn't believe it myself, but that's what I've been told."

I became ragingly infatuated with curiosity at what sins he could've possibly done that has forced him to live an afterlife in which all you know is the moss that clambers up your body, the vines wrapping each limb as your wet cold remains are trapped, and your eyes only see the same treeline, banished from ever seeing the light break over a village wall again.

"Who told you this?" I questioned.

"The wood! She's got her eyes an' ears on everything from here to where the water tips over the edge of the world. Back in my day, I fell under a curse from a particular rune that was given to me. Never was I a man of material possessions; I worked on the fields and gave blood and tears to provide for my family. The summers on which I worked were harsh and the sun had little mercy for field workers like myself. Men would burst in flame while others would go insane from the deceiving rays from the sky. Me? Well I considered myself lucky. I worked senselessly for what felt like a lifetime. I was gifted this rune by a woman; never once did I consider her identity. Her voice seemed eerily familiar, the gentle whispers entrenching their way into my consciousness. The rune had a similar effect on my life as I gradually became besotted with the wooden chip. Such a simple and meaningless item. Such a petty little thing which I became obsessed with. It spoke to me in whispers of a language I didn't seem to recognise. No tongue from this world I know that much. It made me do things; things the mind couldn't comprehend. The body rejected the concepts it presented me, and before I knew it the forest dragged me down here... to be judged and sentenced."

The rhythmic, swirling patterns of movement by the ghastly vision of a man still wondered the dark. With haste I moved, intending to reach Terragoth before next nightfall. It was a goal that was achievable for a select few, however for an unexperienced young Scotsman, the task seemed as complex as painting stars in the sky. The journey became a blur to me, the green vegetation all blending to become one, it was as if I was stuck in a loop stumbling through the same blades of grass, jumping over the same creek, passing through the same stream. With each breath my body grew weary. The ground cried out, pulling me down. Each step became heavier. It wasn't until the moon turned into the sun, that I realised each step was more of an attempt to regain balance, and my eyes had become deceptive, showing me a blurred and spinning image of my surroundings. My left boot stepped, however as it touched the ground, my leg as a support was missing, and my body crumbled under the immense weight of fatigue and misfortune.

Darkness shrouded me, the cries of helplessness and fear give the air the foul stench of death and horror. The sound of cold steel through warm flesh, and the spilling of blood on soil sent shivers down my spine, so forceful I was shocked into battle, two armies clashing both insignias that blessed their shields held no relevance to the blood that was shed. The terrors of war flashed in saturated images that haunted the halls of my fractured memories. The images, of the harrowing faces of men as they breathe their last cry, before their head is taken from their shoulders by the faceless suits of armour. Behind those emotionless helmets lay the souls of men who fight another battle inside them, one which questions their morality, their lives, and their actions, before they spy another, and swing their swords again. The splintering of skulls, the crunch of bones and cries of man have become their rhythm to which they senselessly obey and engage in battle, pleasing death.

A delicate, simple flake of snow gently lands on my skin, immediately becoming a water droplet that runs down my face, waking me from my slumber. I take a knee, my aching bones making the simple act of standing a difficult act itself. However, the subtle snowflakes that weave their way down to the ground meant that I could gladly infer that my journey to the mountains of Terragoth was almost over. I took slow strides, as my legs remembered how to walk. The ground felt tough, the soil becoming solid from the intricate ice that had sunk its way underneath the surface. The foot of the mountain had become visible to me now, as did my breath, which was shunned from the surrounding cold air. Terragoth was not always hidden under a sheet of ice. Years ago, back to the early ages of the world, Terragoth was a utopia, bearing fruit and flower. It remained this way for generations and kings would even wage war for the land to control the ranges. However, what they misunderstood was that Terragoth could feel the bloodshed and animosity that had clouded the pure vision of once great kings. So, winters came. Brutal winters that refused to leave, a constant stream of snow and ice fell over the land and the once beautiful land of Terragoth became a beacon of death, a place where man couldn't die, only be frozen in time and space, never to leave again.

Snow caked the rims of my boots, the cold melted ice finding its way to my feet through the cracks in the battered leather. Shivers became frequent enough I was able to recognise and pre-emptively prepare myself for the cold to shake my spine and make my hairs stand. A minute yet noticeable ache began to build just behind my eyes, the constant white became a tempter into the realms of insanity, one in which I had to occasionally remind myself not to fall in. The light from the sun met the thick white sheet of snow that buried Terragoth, however the heat seemed to become lost in the atmosphere that hovered above the peaks of the range. The air became thin, and no longer nourished my lungs like the air on the ground fed the plants and trees. I had a hard time deciphering how much of it was the thinning of the air, and how much was my body going into in a bitter state of shock because of the constant attack of the cold. I was aimlessly wondering up the mountain without the slightest sense of the location of this cave. The cave that held the supposed cure to the nightmares that visited me each time the moon rose. From my bag I drew a wax candle. An old thing that had been chipped and cracked from its passed uses. It was at this moment I was filled with dread as I fumbled over my words, hoping for the right combination of vowels to leave my dried, cracked lips, to ignite the flame. This item was uniquely crafted back in my homeland. I was not a being of magic heritage, nor was I ever to dip my toes into the pool of the mystic arts, purely for the fear of the destruction it would have on my soul. Magic tears the soul, gives it scars longer than a mountain bear could give you with one swing of its mighty paw. The item held a mystic prowess however it was one I did not question or wish to know more about. As I whispered to the candle stick, the wick gradually blackened as the fragile flame attempted to ember, despite battling the sharp winds. The bombardment of falling snow continued to form in the grey clouds overhead. The flame silently screamed into existence, no bigger than a grain of rice, yet in this land of ice the heat felt like that of a temperate summer's day. The journey became tough and doubt planted its malicious self into my mind, eagerly feeding me thoughts of turning back, to the warm where flowers grew, and trees thrived. These thoughts had little time to manifest as they were shunned by the sight of a cave structure. This was it. My answers were close. My questions were to be diminished. The Cave of Winters.

Chapter 8
Caladrius, the Man in the Wall

If darkness and famine had a scent, this cave was full of it. Using the dim flame from the candle, which at this point had beads of candle wax solidifying on my knuckles, I became acquainted with my surroundings. The wet floor amplified the echoes of the dripping water. The walls, jagged and irregular giving an immense feeling of unease that consumed me quickly. I dabbled in thoughts of leaving the cave, much like I had in the darkness of the alley in freshwater, and the Tomb that housed the Cultists of Jordinn. But common sense suggested that my chances of survival would diminish should I leave to head down the mountain now. The snow fell at such a rate that at the lip of the cave all that could be seen was a wall of white. I held the candle at arm's reach and delved deeper into the darkness. Abruptly after my final step, I came face to face with a sight that baffled me, for lodged in the wall, was a man. Only the ends of his arms and his head protruded from the wall as it clasped him like a clam to a pearl. He was held as if he were a thief or robber in the pillory posts. He appeared to be aged, with few strands of silver hair falling over his face, his face which was in a constant state of being scrunched. Internally, I questioned if this was due to pain, or because the candle I brandished was the only light he had seen in months? Years? Centuries?

"You are not the first to come to me," he said.

His voice croaked in a way I had never been aware existed until then. I half expected dust to cough from his mouth.

"How was your climb up here? That dastard snow still there?"

"Yes, sir, stronger than ever," I replied.

Upon hearing my voice, which was still shaky and recovering from the ice he appeared further enthused. "Ah, a foreigner! What brings you to these parts? Far from home, are you not?"

"Well… I was searching for a witchblood initially. Then I was told she was dead. I am unsure of my purpose now. I was also told you would know about nightmares and dark thoughts?"

"Nightmares? Hmm nightmares… yes, yes. The animals or the visions in your sleep?"

I was unaware that nightmares were creatures. This land was very fascinating to me.

"The ermm… the visions in my sleep, sir."

"Enough with the sir, you can call me Caladrius, distant relative of the God being Autem."

I was in bed, a child of nine at most. I remember my father pulling a book from the shelf that mirrored my bed. The dust on the book was obscene, it was clear that either he favoured other books, or possibly forgot about this one. He sat and read.

"It all began with the will of the Autem, the forger of worlds. At the beginning there was darkness. This darkness flowed like a river through itself and there was peace. The darkness was calm, collective and clever. The darkness

63

continued its reign for billions of years, until, the being we will come to know as Autem, willed himself to life. The darkness was a talented schemer and a being filled with knowledge that no other could possibly possess, god or mortal. The darkness saw its offspring, the being Autem, forged from the darkness itself. Autem looked at his reflection within the darkness, and in the reflection he saw his charcoal black beard and his yellow glowing eyes like the stars. However, he felt a sense of distress. He felt a cloud of confusion within himself and it pained him. Sensing the troublesome nature of its offspring, the darkness plotted. It looked upon its offspring and cradled the man like a mother would her child. It whispered into the ear of the giant man, 'Autem… that is your name. Come, be one with us, and you will have the peace you desire. Watch as we flow in harmony. This was once your home Autem. Return to us.' Autem watched upon the darkness as it moved seamlessly within itself. It was the entity that existed in complete harmony within itself… this tempted Autem, who felt conflict. The darkness felt accomplished and began to take Autem back into the flowing nature of the darkness. Now that Autem was in a state of paralysis it began to strike him. Like a whip the darkness struck its offspring, attempting to kill the virus it had created. One by one the lashings scarred the man's back. However, he would not die. Autem awoke. The offspring of the darkness felt an anger build within him, for it was his nature to feel emotion, conflict, and anger. The two beings began to strike each other. One for one, their blows boomed within the darkness. The darkness, feeling the growing rage and power of their offspring, cursed the man. They cursed him with eternal life, forcing the confused and conflicted being to continue living in his curse of emotional discomfort for an infinite number of years. Angered by this, the eternal being Autem grabbed his left arm. He tore into his own flesh and bone, the pain searing through his body. He screamed at the curse he now had to bear. He had little knowledge of the many powers and magic of the darkness and feared that the curse be true. From his disfigured and bloody arm, he pulled his radius bone and from it he created a battle axe with which contained the same forbidden power and magic of the darkness. With this axe he dealt the finishing blow to the darkness forever ridding it from this universe."

"Forger of worlds..." I said in disbelief.

Caladrius the man in the wall was a descendant of Autem, who himself was a myth?

"Your nightmares. Please, explain," he enquired.

I could feel his words cutting through my barriers, spilling open my words containing the information of the nightmares that visited me each night.

"Why?"

"You pose a question that holds many answers, young man. Nightmares prey on vessels for their power. You – what's your name?"

"John Sawyer."

"Yes, yes, well, John. Are you afraid?"

"Yes."

"What brings you fear?"

"This place. I feel a daunting pressure. I feel an immense force that disperses through my being, assimilating all signs of life within me. I feel myself becoming nothing more than that vessel of nightmares."

"How interesting. John, you must understand, I can only lead you down the path. The end has already been written in the stars of fate. You will go to the capital. The city of Amor Ceriel."

Yet again I was being led to another place. Another travel. Another journey. Every second I spent in the wildland, I felt ages pass. I felt unease. My fists clenched, turning white. "But... I-I was promised answers! What is this endless chase for the truth? The city of Amor Ceriel will lead me elsewhere, where no answers will flourish. I am being trapped in this place, searching for something that doesn't exist!" Immediately after, I felt regret for my outburst, however this didn't seem to faze Caladrius. Instead he simply sighed and looked down at the floor in despair.

"You have a purpose to fulfil, Sawyer. Have faith. Head to Amor Ceriel."

Time passed in an irregular and random pattern in the cave. When I had first stepped foot onto the wet rock and gaseous air, it had been daylight for very few hours. However, the night was not fleeting, it was persistent. The gentle illuminous glow of the moon lit the lip of the cave, only just, so you could bathe your feet in the light. Caladrius moaned of how he missed the world. The chirping of birds, the conversing of crickets, the gentle breeze that you long for on a hot summer's morn. The rock had been his prison for many years. His ears had become accustom to the shrieks of bats as they fluttered slightly below the ceiling of the cave. His eyes accommodated the dark and he joked that the dark was even more kind than the light.

"My eyes haven't rested on the light of my home in what feels like eternities," I said, as memories of home still ran amok throughout my head.

"The light in your land is the same light here."

"No, it's different. This light is harsh. Like everything in this place, even the light feels like it's trying to achieve some sort of harm."

"I guessed you would come to that conclusion," Caladrius said as a smug smile came over his face, the first smile I had seen since I arrived in the cave.

To be able to see into the mind of this man would be too immense for a mortal to cope, although I was far too intrigued. I wished desperately to know my journey. Partly for curiosity, partly because I selfishly wished to control my own fate. I didn't like the idea that my destiny was pre-determined.

Stories of the great city of Amor Ceriel reached even the ears of my Scottish neighbours back home. Of how the masonry of each tower, and each building was so precise and specific, that the buildings stood strong for hundreds of years without fault. The centre of the city housed a great tower where the great King Ichilla reigned over his kingdom. The tower itself was protected by a rather large serpent who coiled its body around it. The serpent wasn't a giant, nor did it have any influence from magic. It was simply just a serpent who didn't stop growing. And according to Caladrius, this is where I was next meant to visit on my path. The words spoken by the illusive Caladrius, the man in the wall, resonated with me. Learning that I had a journey, I had a path and a purpose calmed me. I knew I had a linear path, of which if I followed, eventually life would return to normality and I would be able to return home. I simply had to fulfil my purpose in this land.

I had originally been under the impression that my mission was to hand the rune over to Cassandra Boyle, the witchblood. However, by the words of the man in the wall, I had a bigger purpose. I waited in the cave until dawn-break. The night passed slowly, in a calm manner, one in which I could think clearly. I could delve deep into my subconscious and begin to work out who I was, and what my purpose was in this strange land. The snoring of Caladrius made this no easy task, his big inhales, and even larger exhales, made sure that my mind couldn't fully expand into realms of the unknown as much as I had intended. I left the cave, in a new light. With a new purpose. I was to go to Amor Ceriel.

Chapter 9
The Whispering Throne

The city itself was visible from far out, while I was still on the foot of Terragoth. Its beauty as it devoured the light in the area was astonishing. The green fields that surrounded the city, were flourishing with butterflies of all sorts, and the occasional honeybee would buzz over to perch on a nearby petal. The city itself was grand. Its architecture was revolutionary, using both wood, steel, and stone to create structures worthy of kings. The buildings scaled larger than the buildings in Burncorn or Freshwater. I felt like a dwarf as I walked around the city in awe. Its city walls thick enough to catch a boulder in mid throw and the city guards brandishing armour that put dragon scales to shame. The spires of lone standing towers reached high into the sky, tall enough that they became lost to my vision. Amor Ceriel was not a place I had intended on visiting. I had heard too many stories of the wildlands and the city that I dared not think of overstaying my welcome. People swarmed the city in bundles, some held status wearing velvet clothes with brass buttons and a tall collar to cover their neck. Others simply wore whatever rags they could use as clothes. The diverse stature of the city meant that I fit in well, none could tell of my heritage, and that I was in fact very very far from home. Deep in the inner circle of

Amor Ceriel, the outside howls, groans, and shrieks were virtually silent, so much I almost forgot that just outside the thick city walls, ghosts, ghouls, and demons were waiting. While pacing around, I found a step on which I perched, still curious about my being in Amor Ceriel and my purpose here? I was told by Caladrius that my journey was to lead me here, however for what reason still baffled me. In this city of many, my mind couldn't seem to grasp what difference I would make? As I sat and pondered on this question I myself put forward, I was approached by a young girl who sat beside me.

"Ello, mister," she said in an accent only one born and bred in the city could possess.

"Hello."

"You, an exorcist?"

"No?" I replied, slightly confused.

I had become very sceptical of all the happenings and goings on, expecting everything to somehow relate to this journey I had been told to follow. I felt as though Caladrius was peering over my shoulder, whispering, beckoning me to take each opportunity that would allow me to take further steps on my 'path'.

"Ugh, well you gots to help me anyway," she replied, grabbing my arm tugging on it like a dog would a bone.

"Child, I don't think I can."

She chose to ignore my doubts continuing to drag me down a street. The area she took me wasn't as grand as the inner city. It held many stalls and markets selling trinkets of all sorts and many holding mystical abilities that people would not be accustom to. It was on this street, that a group of men approached adjacent from a stool which housed an old man crooked and bent at the waist.

"Stop! You are wanted by the king," shouted a brute near the back of the group, as they sped down what remained of the street, and grabbed my arm just like the girl did moments prior.

The men wore armour, however not the armour of a knight, no. It was a simple breastplate, one that hugged the neck and waist tight, and seemed to balloon out around the midsection. An insignia of what appeared to be a red hammer, on a white tree had been carelessly slapped on with a paint that chipped and faded. This meant there was little more than a red mark on their armour. Despite this, I followed the men without question. If this was where my path was to take me, then so be it. The girl also persisted on following us, she walked a few paces behind and was muttering expletives to herself about how this was unfair, and that these men were poor excuses of guards of Amor Ceriel. The girl seemed to know more than me if she was aware who the men were. Turning yet another corner in the maze of architecture, we arrived at the keep. I was stood just underneath where the great serpent hugged the watch tower tightly. The men loosened their grip on my arm now; apparently, they had convinced themselves that I posed no threat, and they were right. The great doors of the keep Amor Ceriel, slowly creaked open, the immeasurable weight putting great strain on the hinges, causing a crunch and squeal to radiate throughout the lower levels of the city. The crunch of metal on metal, brought glimpses of now buried memories to resurface. The red blood splatters, the clanging of steel and the screams of men. Evidentially I was visibly disturbed for one of the guards, a skinnier man whose chest plate was far too big for him, prodded my shoulder.

"You all right, sir?" he mumbled.

"Yes. Yes, I'm fine. Just having some thoughts."

"Well, you might wanna hold those thoughts when your face to face with Ichilla."

"Ichilla? What does he want with me?"

I posed questions to the skinny man hoping some sort of sympathy would transpire and he might give me some answers. His lips opened, but rather than words forming, he simply let out an irritated exhale and turned his sight back towards the doors, which by now had been opened. The hall in which we entered held a far superior architectural desire than the surrounding city. The walls were plated in gold with silver seams running throughout. From the ceiling, which was higher than any tree I had before seen, hung purple banners, strung from each side of the room. Opposite where we had just entered, was a throne, made from wood but from the top protruded antler like wooden pikes. It held carvings of sacred runes throughout which gave a gentle sun like glow, so subtle one wouldn't be able to see it, unless they searched. Even from the far side of the hall we could hear the vacant whispers of the runes. What they were saying I was unsure; many mortal ears were not made to hear such whispers unless they were of royal decent. The King of Amor Ceriel slumped on the throne, his eyes closed listening ever so closely to the whispers of the throne. We approached in silence, not even the men who abducted me from the marketplace dared speak a word. Each step was taken in silence. We were simply a few steps from the throne, and the king himself, before without any sort of context given to me, one of the men gave me a slight shove forward.

"Ah! Good-morning, gentlemen!" said Ichilla, opening his eyes and greeting me with his arms wide.

He wore black velvet which complimented his dirty blonde hair. He leapt from his throne and hugged me tight, only like a mother would do to her child, or like my father did to me. Standing, he appeared tall, however less stocky than the brute who brought me here. His hair was long and fair and drawn back behind his ears which were jewelled. Some called Ichilla 'two eyes' because his left was a sea blue and his right was a deep sepia. While in a state of awe with so much I wanted to ask and say, Ichilla continued,

"I trust your journey here hasn't been too rough? You did come from Scotland, right?"

He proceeded to put his arm around me, and we walked out of hall by a side passage leading to beautiful gardens. The light in the gardens differed from the light that fell upon the rest of the earth. The yellow tint was absent and instead a light of pure white blessed the vegetation which gently swayed in the kind breeze. Few insects and animals inhabited the area that I could see, yet the hymns of birds, joined with the chirping of crickets was sheer bliss. I'm unsure how much time passed as I was captivated by the beauty of the garden, but it was long enough for Ichilla to further ask, "Your journey?"

"Oh yes, yes… sorry. Erm. I have past Freshwater, Burncorn and my travels also took me to the mountains of Terragoth."

"That sounds… intriguing," he said with much interest woven between his words gently caressing his stubble.

"What's your name?" asked the king.

This further added to my confusion, the man seemed to know so much about me, yet so little.

"J—John," I said.

"Ah well, John. We have a lot to speak of. Let's talk."

"You see, John, I'm sure you've spent long enough in this land now to realise it's not the same as your dear country. You've seen how the land contorts and conforms to became treacherous. It has fallen into darkness. Its unfaithful. The distrust comes with the cloak the land wears. It will show you the Tree with golden bark, its branches holding leaves greener than greenest green. Behind the physical aspects to which we are drawn, lies a dagger ready to plunge deep into the hearts of man. The land has even brought curses from hell itself. A century's worth of curses that fall on the land as frequent as rain. It's a dangerous place to be. Now I'm sure your wondering, John, where do you fit in this?"

I gave a vacant nod, transfixed by the words of the king.

"My throne. It's been whispering to me, it always does. These whispers are different though. They no longer entice me with rumours of this great city and the wise words of wisdom from the Gods. No, they began to speak to me of a man. I thought I had drunk too much ale when it began. They spoke of a man not from this land. A man who would change the tides of destiny of this land. They spoke of how the land would once again thrive, not on shadows and fear, but on hope and light. I believe you are this man, John."

The herald kept a face of sincerity while mine dropped to a face of shock and fear. The fear instilled in me of this land was one that was genuine. I remembered being curled up on the dirt and grass, the storm raging. Flashes of lightning lit up the tears that fell from my face, and the thunder echoed permanently in my ears.

The conversation ended shortly after with Ichilla noticing that I would need some time to accept this role as a saviour of the wildlands. I sat on a bench in the gardens staring at an ant on the floor. I pictured how the ant was out finding food to feed its family. It would clamber over blades of grass like I would mountains, avoiding the dangers of beetles and other creatures that would threaten it. It would scamper into unknown holes and crevasses in the land almost fearlessly, not even considering the consequences simply because the ant knew how strong and capable it was. And when it finally found food, the ant would rush back home, trampling over anything that attempted to stop it. I was nothing like the ant. I was scared. Terrified for if I failed, I would never see my land again. As I rose from the bench, a dizziness came over me, I assumed because I was deep in thought. I stumbled back into the hall and the whispering of the throne became apparent yet again. To my dismay, they were still in a language forbidden to the ears of man. However, despite this I could still decrypt the vowels of my name. I felt as though the throne was speaking of me though I was unaware to whom. I ambled in the direction of the throne, at a slow pace so I could further analyse the noises that emanated from the wooden seat of Ichilla.

"Sir?"

A voice from behind me came, which drowned out the whispers of the throne. I turned and was presented with the young girl again.

"Is you, gonna help me, then?" she demanded.

It was clear she wasn't informed what I was, or what Ichilla believed I was.

"I… I was just—"

"It's all right! I won't tell mister what's his face you was lookin at his chair," she interrupted.

The innocence in her voice was simply a juxtaposition from her scruffy street demeanour.

"You seek the help of an exorcist? I am not who you are searching for young one."

"Don't 'young one' me, old man. Listen, I'm err… I will be straight with you. I ain't got the money to hire an exorcist. But you're the next best thing, right? My auntie lives in Burncorn; she says yous went to the East woods and came out without a scratch."

At this point I got a twitch in my neck, an awkward twitch as I looked away in despair. This young lady perceived me as a hero of sorts. Could I inform her and shatter her expectations of me? Inform her of the nightmares, nightmares that are ever present in my dreams and follow me into reality where daylight shines? Could I tell her of the incident at the tomb of the cult of Jordinn, how I fled from the battle, a blubbering mess as men, who weren't evil simply misguided, were slew, their blood seeping between the stoned floor and into the soil deep below.

Instead I said, "What's the problem?" and took another step down the path.

Chapter 10
The Burning

The young girl refused to let go of my hand as she dragged me to show me the problem with which she required the assistance of an Exorcist. I was certain that my skills were inferior to what was needed but I was willing to see if I could help in any way. As she stormed through the maze of concrete she was mumbling, her words incoherent, though I was sure she was speaking English. She took me far from the spires that were huddled around the cities keep, down into the areas of Amor Ceriel that were dark, damp and never meant to be seen by any, let alone a man from a foreign land. It was this part of the city that was shadowed by the spires. The giant prowess of stone masonry. This part held those who had nothing. The people were run down, many of them ragged. Scrapes and bruises covering them, it was nigh impossible to find a patch of skin that was untouched by dirt, blood, or cuts. It was these parts that the earth had begun to reclaim, prying the rocks apart to make room for hordes of vines and weeds. These vines then began to crawl towards the light slithering up the side of the nearby buildings. I couldn't place it, but there also appeared to be a dark fog in the area, unseen by those who already belonged there. The girl didn't seem phased as I was, therefore, I had come to the likely assumption that she was a person who belonged here.

"Don't let it bother ya. These guys are harmless," she muttered.

As she spoke, I felt many eyes on me, the quietly judging eyes of the people from the area. I felt dirty to wear fur and leather, unworthy to brandish a belt with steel. I was led to a small room, behind an old wood door, infested with rot and insects. The incessant moans from the room were unpleasant and repulsive, making my further steps into the room a task. In the room was a chair, and on the chair was the source of the noises. It was a woman. She remained still enough for a fly to befriend her, yet her slow raspy breathing was harrowing. Streams of saliva dripped from her mouth; her head drooped towards the floor.

"Can you help her?" the girl enquired.

Slowly advancing towards the woman, panic struck as I quickly became very aware of how stuffy it was in the room, and how I had no idea what I was doing. Luckily, fear is an intense and powerful motivator. Each step I took without question. I was determined since Caladrius, Terragoth, and since speaking with Ichilla that my destiny was set. These were simply my first steps into a bigger life. I reached a hand out, unsure of my actions. Gently I touched her arm, and I was thrown into darkness.

I found myself in a forest, one of many in the land of green. The seas of night were in the sky, and the light was shunned from every leaf, twig and mound in the woods. It was silent enough to hear the taps of a spider's legs on the mossy damp ground. I was confused more than frightened as I senselessly searched for the room with the woman in the chair. Maybe I had been shifted here by magic? Maybe it's all an illusion? A deep regret surfaced, as I realised that perhaps I should've consulted with Ichilla or even an exorcist before stepping foot into that room, before seeing that woman. Some of the far trees quickly became silhouettes, a bright orange glow radiated from behind. Convinced the light was from the sun, I raced towards it. Each leap and bound, my feet gradually sunk further into the dingy wet ground. Upon the glowing tree line, a great fire raged. The trees screeching for help as their bark turned to black and the inferno engulfed them. They shared the same fate, unable to uproot and run, trapped in place. They stand unwilling, and afraid as the fire took them. Even the leaves attempted to flee, falling from the branches, riding the wind to safety, but the embers too flew on the wind. Creatures emerge from their holes in the ground and run from the monster squealing and crying. The shrieks from the helpless animals fall upon absent ears, as my senses are otherwise occupied with the flame as it danced atop its prey and the smoke as it joined the night sky. Burning. It was only then I saw the burning of the woods, the burning of the wildlands and most certainly the most fearsome thing of all… The burning of Amor Ceriel. I was thrown again, and came to my senses, panting in a puddle of sweat or tears of which I was unsure. The girl with her hand on my shoulder.

"Mister, are you okay?"

"Ye… yes. What happened? What did she do to me?"

My hostility came across clearly.

"She did nothing, sir. You fixed her! Gotta have some sort of magic touch!"

"B… but…" I said in confusion, however she pondered on words, that eventually spoke,

"You did mumble a bit though. I only really understood one or two words. Gotta be magic ha-ha." She giggled.

"Thought I was gonna have to get you an exorcist too!"

"What… what did I say?" I asked.

She looked at me, the glee turning to a sincerity.

"Just somethin about burning…"

I spent more time that night staring at the cracks in the beams along the ceiling than I ever had before. The little inefficient distraction that I hoped would stop my mind pondering on the events that had transpired over the past few hours. Each and every second brought back through my memories. I was being dragged deep to a place I loathed, to a place I hated… to a place I feared. To a place I tried to avoid every moment the sun was in the sky. It was a place I had become far too familiar with. A place where what you perceive is meaningless, for the end is always the same. The end will always be the tears in your eyes, the clammy palms and the ants in your head making you want to scream, cry or weep. This was that place. I never wanted to end up there. But moments like that, staring up to the ceiling, as the waning light of the moon crept through the windowpane, was a moment that would become inevitably engulfed by the immense feelings of sadness, fear and hopelessness. It would become my dread. My own personal dread. The nightmare that came in my consciousness before it then seeped into my dreams and plagued them with the same harrowing feelings of darkness. It was a nightmare that followed me wherever I went. And happiness had left my side and I was introduced with a new acquaintance known as anguish. An acquaintance that would never leave me, unlike happiness. An acquaintance I would come to know very well.

What was I to do? I knew I had purpose, that I had meaning, I was convinced of it. I knew that purpose was to purge the wildlands to bring prosperity to a land that was to flourish and once again would a rose be able to grow within the soil without harm being bequeathed upon it. I was the one who was to banish the evil and bring forth the light that was to shine even on the darkest of nights, to shine among the great light of the stars that littered the sky in patterns and swirls that the mind couldn't comprehend. I knew my duty. This vision and this haunting by the woman in the cellar. I believed it was the fear of failure that instilled the Burning vision upon me. This was what to happen if I failed my destiny. The plains would burn, the cities would fall and the world would crumble. The pressure returned; its distinct heavy presence was one that I recognised. It was an immense feeling of being dragged down with a secondary feeling of fear gradually swelling beneath. It was one I knew all too well. But… fear is a great motivator. I was sure I wouldn't let the world burn. I would fulfil my destiny. I would purge the evil curse of the wildlands.

I went to the throne room to accept the offer given by Ichilla on that fateful day. Upon entering the hall, a man passed by, his eyes barely joining with mine before glancing away and hastily making an exit. His appearance matched the brief description Yen gave to me of Sir Nash, the vicious ruler of Burncorn a lifetime ago. Ichilla had a small, yet noticeable sweat. The light shone on his forehead with a few strands of his fair hair sticking to his forehead. However, telling Ichilla of the news that I had chosen to accept this fate made him euphoric to say the least. His grin bigger than his mouth would allow, as he bounced around the throne room like a child in hysteria.

He shouted at all the guards, "Yes, our saviour is here!" as they continued to stare forward with little emotion.

I had chosen to keep the burning vision private. I fear what someone with the power of Ichilla would do if he knew that I saw his city fall.

Ichilla gleefully spoke, "Yes, see now we know you've accepted your fate; I do have a task for you."

"Of course," I spoke hastily without thought.

"Tomorrow, when the moon rises it will bleed red. This will beckon forth a creature. We have received news from a neighbouring village, Thornfief, of this creature. They smell its revolting stench on the air. The smell of dried blood and burning coal, a scent that fills the noses of the many people living in Thornfief. I believe, John…" he said gripping my hand tight, "… the slaying of this beast will mark the beginning of our… your journey."

There was a silence in the room as Ichilla looked at me with a helpless and kind look. The kind a friend would give you when they asked a favour. Ichilla was a man I had known for little time, but he had vision. He had ideals and ideas for the great city of Amor Ceriel and I passionately believed that this progression would bring peace and light back to the wildlands. I trusted him.

So, I spoke, "Then this beast will come to know the pain it has caused others."

Before I journeyed to Thornfief, Ichilla led me down into the chambers deep in the keep of Amor Ceriel. He explained how these chambers were the staple of the city. The roar of the torch flame gave a gentle ominous echo behind the voice of Ichilla.

"Down here we have books and inscriptions that were written before the first witchblood uttered her first words. We have weapons too dastardly for the hands of man. What is here is yours, brother."

He hugged me, before clambering back up the spiral staircase we descended just moments before. I briefly looked around the room – I didn't want to invade the privacy of King Ichilla, despite what he said. Next to the spears and Warhammer's I found a sword that took my liking. I felt a certain draw to it, similar to the whispering throne. The sword was half my height, light weight and its blade greased and sharpened ready to draw blood.

I read the inscription on the side of the scabbard; it read: 'Till your dying breath.'

The chambers were cold, making my hands fumble and shake as I flipped through the crinkled stained parchment, each with scribbles of ink splashed over it back to front. I thought if I searched for the term 'Bleeding moon' I might learn of this creature, the one who smelt of dried blood and coal. Turning page after page, I read of a creature known as Snare. Snare was a monster of terror; whose tales of pillage reached the ears of young children to make them behave. It was a large snake like being who slithered over the mounds and hills with scales of iron. However, the torso of the snare, was a furry body similar to that of a were-beast with scars, the reminders of past encounters with humans who attempted to kill it before. Long horns curled from its forehead and it's said that the horns were pulled from its skull by the darkness itself. Upon learning of my foe, what little confidence I possessed was shunned from my thoughts. I ran my hands through my hair, looking over at my chosen sword again. 'Until your dying breath.' This was to be the time Snare wouldn't leave with scars. I would tear its horns out myself. Until my dying breath.

Chapter 11

Fellows of Thornfief

The journey to Thornfief was swift and simple. Its neighboured close to Amor Ceriel and was the second largest settlement behind the great city itself. I rode into the village on a horse gifted to me by Ichilla himself. The horse's saddle was uncomfortable and threw me every way possible; however its uses became clear upon entering the village where I was hailed by many as I bore the insignia of Amor Ceriel. I was quickly approached by a woman, short and stocky as many women of the military were.

"You come from the city?" she enquired, standing tall to attention, almost as if she were trying to look me in the eyes as I was seated on my horse.

"Yes. I have been told of the bleeding moon and the creature who stalks these parts."

The woman nodded, before whispering to one of her fellow officers and led me to the keep of the village. Upon first glance many would see the village as normal, with a thriving marketplace, hardworking citizens and a structure to the town that made sure it would stand for centuries. All these observations would be correct, however there was more to the city than one could imagine. The military of the city was cunning, collective and their strategy was unmatched. Thornfief may not have bred the strongest warriors, however they were smart and many dared not face them. I was shown to my room, while the woman made sure I was informed of the directions around the keep. My horse was taken to the stapled and likewise, I was taken to my room.

"You can rest here, until the calling of the monster."

"Thank you for your hospitality," I said.

And when the wooden door slammed shut, I thoughtlessly switched back to the person I once was as I swept sweat from my brow. I feared the oncoming battle, however the people of Thornfief needed hope, especially if they were aware of my place in the prophecy spoken by the Whispering Throne of Amor Ceriel. The fear I felt was pre-destined to strike exactly at this time and place as it sat on the silk bedding, fumbling my hands. There did seem to be an underlying presence of confidence though, like a netting catching me from falling into darkness, as I had done so many times before. This was the presence of those words spoken by Ichilla. I was the one to prosper the wildlands. This instilled hope in me. Maybe this battle with the snare wouldn't prove to be as big of a task as was given by Ichilla. I lay in the bed, sleepless yet again, wondering of the place I was in. I had heard little of Thornfief, only of how the village was impenetrable. From my window in the keep, I gazed upon the rest of the buildings and constructs of the rest of the town. The rows of beige tiles seemed endless with houses tightly condensed into the city gates. The night had drawn people back to their houses and the streets seemed bare, like a tree who had shed its leaves. Compared to what I had seen before, I was surprised to see each row of houses so easily with no one in sight except the odd soldier pacing around the maze of concrete who would occasionally wobble as they were almost taken by sleep. The door rattled and into my abode arrived the woman from earlier.

"How are you feeling?" she asked, joining me to peer out upon the village.

My silence invited her to speak further.

"If you look carefully, you might be able to see the glow from the lights of Amor Ceriel. Such a vast city, eh?" she said.

"Yes, yes I suppose so. I hadn't seen such a city even at home."

"Of course you're not from around here are you?"

"No. And this beast who will arrive at the bleeding moon. Nor does his kind reside in my lands."

As if the moon had listened to my thoughts and my words, a deep red came over it. Slowly it dripped down the white glow and gradually a new pale red colour painted the landscape. Each street in Thornfief had succumb to madness, as the red reached the eyes of the awake and the minds of the dreaming. Screams and derelict cries reached the ears of those in the keep.

"Your foe has arrived," the woman said, as a damp smell of dried blood wafted through the great halls of the keep.

I grasped the hilt of my blade and strapped it to my side. Yet again, the face of John filled with dread was cast aside. That was not the man who could fulfil this task. I had to become John, the saviour of the wildlands. I became determined with an underlying fear. The fear of failure was ever present however the vision of the snares head mounted on my blade was powerful.

I left the town, each stride I could feel my blade clinking in the scabbard, thirsty to taste the blood of the beast. I had little idea which direction I would have to go to find the snare and would be forced to simply follow my nose. With each mound or dip in the grass I came to, I halted before sniffing at the wind like a mutt. The smell first filled my nose, to which I was repulsed however, the closer I got it began to find its way to my lungs forcing me to keel over gagging and vomiting. I had never envisioned the stench having such a strong effect. However, I was certain the beast would feel my steel in its flesh. The ground gradually dipped into a clearing in which I first laid eyes on the Snare. I watched as its snake like body coiled up with its greenish scales each placed not to reveal any soft flesh. I deduced the reasoning for the smell that was by now, so fierce the grass had begun to wilt in the area that the snare lay was due to the fur of the beast. The fur which had been soaked in blood of innocence and the saliva of the snare himself, who licked his wounds from foes who had before attempted to stop his reign of terror under the blood weeping moon. To my untrained eye, the beast looked as though he was simply slithering around the clearing, flattening the grass underneath him, never to stand again. Like any hunter would do, I slowly moved down the hill, under the cover of the red night, which apparently was still dim enough to not be seen by the animal. I was fast and possibly first to learn, that the snare was far from an animal. When I got close behind, the snare turned, slowly so I could look into his glowing yellow eyes as he growled a fowl growl, and from it I managed to decipher the words,

"Man? Master? Another human to fall upon these grounds. I will paint the moon in your blood."

The land was still and silent. The depths of night had calmed the plains. Blood light from the moon, still waned across the fields and forests, illuminating each leaf and each blade of grass in new shades which would flummox the commoner. Even the gentle winds guided from the west respected the silence and further calmed to become little more than a breeze. However, this sound was suddenly interrupted with the clash of steel and shrieks from a creature so evil, only hell could've spat it out. The snare rushed me, quick to put its claws on my throat. Instinctively I raised my drawn blade. The clash from the claw on blade vibrated my whole being. My knees felt wobbly and my stomach dropped. I stumbled to find my footing as the monster proceeded to slither around me growling and baring its teeth. My thoughts of confidence, of taking the head of the animal back to Thornfief, returning as a hero were briefly questioned. The snare postured itself yet again before striking. My raised sword defence failed me this time for the long snake tail of the beast whipped from behind and I fell to the grass. *I considered staying down and playing dead perhaps? Maybe the Snare would just leave? No*, I thought. I rushed to my feet, raising my sword yet again. The antiphysic movements of the creature was vastly unlike a man. I remembered the simple, yet effective techniques my father showed me when I was a young lad. Keep your stance, watch for patterns and body positioning. I considered the effectiveness of such techniques against an opponent who was as tall as a tree and possessed a scaled tail that would make blows from my sword little more than pinches from a child.

The snare slobbered and foamed, grizzling, "Do you feel afraid?"

Before lunging again, this time his tail clattering my blade from my grip. Panicked I lashed out for I was afraid. I was terrified of this beast but it wasn't that he mocked me for it that made my blood boil. It was that he knew. I forgot about the sword that was plugged into the dirt paces from me and I threw my fists. The unexpected attack meant each punch connected with the beast's face. I didn't hold back and I had no intentions of stopping until the Snare moved no more. I became unaware of my actions, as if my sanity and consciousness left my body, leaving nothing but a vessel of anger driven by deep fear cultivated by anxiety. By the time I became aware and in control again, my hands were bloody. For a short amount of time I searched my body for any lacerations or deep wounds but none were found. Instead, I saw the Snare with one of its horns, snapped and implanted firmly in the top of its skull. Yet again, I was in the presence of the familiarity of the pale light of the moon, the blood colour banished to hell with the monster formally known as the Snare as I stood atop of his corpse growing cold by the second. Despite the lack of danger now that the monster's eyes were rolled and his blood was feeding the parched land, my knees felt weaker than before. I knew of the innocent life that this beast had taken and I knew of its intentions should it have won the battle. But the memories surfacing of the scrap, brought back the whimpers of the Snare as I dug its own horn deep in-between its eyes. Rationality never showed itself at these times, as I was left crying by the dead body of a monster. My breathing became rapid, despite my tries to slow it and reach a state where I could stand without buckling.

"It's okay, John, it's okay," I assured myself. "This is what's meant to happen. This is all part of Ichilla's plan. It's okay. It's okay."

The fractured images of the violence continued to plague my vision, until one final vision presented itself, but not of the battle nor the Snare. It was Caladrius. Then peace befell the land again. The wind continued to blow, unaware of the loss of the beast that wondered it minutes ago. The trees continued to stand and wave gracefully, despite the change of light on their leaves. And even I had become very aware of the silence. My breathing was loud and raspy, my heart was thudding but when I noticed the deathly silence that haunted the area, I too was beckoned to join it. I stood again, calm and collected like I was part of the land. I walked over to the hilt that was like a tree stump in the ground. I drew it, the words engraved lit by the moonlight. The events that led to this moment seemed foreshadowing and I had an inkling that I knew how this journey would close. I had to visit Caladrius again, his seemingly infinite wisdom and knowledge about a life that he didn't possess fascinated me and I had a considerable number of questions to pose him. I saw Caladrius as a trusted being. He reminded me of my father.

The journey back to Thornfief felt long without the assistance of a horse and even longer while dragging the decapitated head of a Snare behind me. By now, the sun had woken and had begun to take the moons place in the sky as the stars retreated back to heaven. The glow of a new dawn lit through the dew drops slowly dripping down the rim of an amber leaf. Even the breeze that glided through the wildlands throughout the night died with it. I could feel the gentle warmth on the back of my head as I followed my shadow forward searching for the path back to Thornfief. The decomposing head held a gathering of flies feeding on the strands of flesh that dangled from the jagged cuts. I was never a butcher, nor an executioner, so my cuts weren't clean but forceful and aggressive. However, this didn't seem to faze the inhabitants of Thornfief who, upon arrival, greeted me with quiet cheers and thanks all while spitting on the head which I still dragged behind me leaving a trail of smeared blood on the stoned floor. Back at the keep, a man who too was seated on a throne, however this one was less grand and didn't whisper, greeted me. I didn't have to be a genius to know that this was the nobleman of Thornfief.

"Ahh, John, is it? I met with Ichilla recently, he informed me you would be arriving."

"Yes, I bring you a… gift I suppose."

"Head of a snare? Well you must be a warrior born and bred!"

The gent leaned in close, close enough to whisper without wondering ears able to listen, "He told me who you really are John. This won't be your first kill John?"

I shook my head, which influenced a grin to grow from the corner of the man's mouth.

"I'm Marr-on. I am the head of Thornfief. I see you met my commanding officer Miss Alina."

The woman who had led me to my room before, I recognised her as she gave me a friendly smile, her face turning a slight shade of red. I tried to keep my words minimal, knowing that I had to get to Terragoth soon to revisit Caladrius.

"Listen, John," he went on. "I feel we must discuss Ichilla's plans."

"I apologise, Marr-on. I must go. I have urgencies. I have… I have…"

"That's okay, John. I'm sure you have pressures to deal with. Off you go, be sure to remember us though…"

Chapter 12

Deviations of Sanity

What is the measure of a man's mind? Wealth can be measured through coin or seen through the grand and masterful craft of castles, that hold more elegance than a swan on a lake. But for the mind of man? What is it that is considered 'wealth'? Happiness? Joy? Or do I delve deeper into the great depths of the imagination of man, where dark thoughts spawn and the ideas of lunacy become apparent. Could this be true wealth? Where the chains of morality are stripped from my aching bones and the madness can inhabit every inch of my being? In this place where the devil himself can be seen walking the same path as I, maybe madness isn't such a bad thing. Maybe, it could be a tool with which I could reform and rebirth the wildlands bringing forth a new age of glory, unity and prosperity. And when I opened my eyes to see the blood dripping between my fingers, perhaps it was madness with which I owed my life. The being with which I cannot see, nor touch. But I can feel the gentle push over the edge to a dark place where not even a glimpse of light, like a pinprick of starlight in the nights sky can be seen. But it saved me. To that I owed thanks.

After being deep in thought for what felt like an eternity, I sat staring into nothingness and concluded that I was due another visit to Caladrius. I knew I had many more questions to pose to him and although he may have refused a lot of my queries, any more knowledge was sacred to me. The day in Thornfief was bright and merry, a day the many people of the village hadn't seen during the reign of the blood moon. The sun shone brighter and the laughs were more prominent to the ears of Marr-on and myself, for which he thanked me profusely. As soon as I stepped through the gateway back into the unknown, a great shudder fell down my spine. It was a shudder that refused to leave and one that stuck around like a foul smell. I couldn't help but fear the journey back to Terragoth; the village of Thornfief was further from the base of the mountains than Amor Ceriel was. I felt a strong disturbance in the grounds, as the grass felt thicker than before, each blade of grass gripped to the underside of my boot and the wind was cunning, swirling and battering against the route I was on. I could almost hear the giggling in the rustling of the trees mocking me. They would lean towards each other and whisper tales of poor man John on the journey they wish to make impossible. Still, I persisted.

I entered the cave, quietly speaking to the ember on the candlestick again which became more confident as I stumbled deeper towards Caladrius.

"Ahhh… If it isn't, John, right?" he spoke with his wise eyes closed, and his limp body still hanging from the wall where I saw him last.

"Caladrius…"

"You're different, boy, you... you smell different," Caladrius said, his head tilting up and smelling the air, as I stood silent.

"You, ohh. You, haha... you have blood on your hands now, don't ya?"

"I killed the bloodmoon snare from Thornfief," I said somewhat proudly without the intent.

"Of course, you did. Following Ichilla's plans closely I see?"

"It was the path I was told to follow by you. Ichilla is using me to bring this land to greatness."

"No, no don't involve me in your plans. I told you, you have a journey that is all. Hmm…"

I waited as Caladrius was seemingly in deep thought; I waited for one of his thoughts to become apparent.

"Isn't it funny? I can hear the Whispering Throne from here."

"You can understand it?"

"I can understand 'her'. It takes a certain type of mind to understand the Whispering Throne of Amor Ceriel."

I took a seat on the stone floor, my ears tuned out the howling of the wind outside the cave and I became transfixed by the poetry of Caladrius.

"I'm old enough that even the oak trees in the depths of the forest call to me to father them. I know each star by name and watched as this land evolved from a damp grassland to an empire of people… and I know of distant lands, some which many would believe could only exist in the vast, ever expanding imaginations of writers or artists. I remember hearing of a tale and I know now that you're ready to hear it. There was once a Kingdom of Glass. The architects claimed that into their dreams of wealth and other material possessions leaked the idea of the Kingdom of Glass. The architects gathered, stroking their beards deep in thought of the perhaps impossible idea. The dream that would become a reality. Through their struggle, they gave their blood and years from their lives to bring forth the Kingdom of Glass from their dreams. It was a spectacle. Every night the sun would set and both the auburn light from the sun and the waning light of the moon would shine through each tower of glass. The light would refract and reflect around the kingdom and children would chase the wonderful display of colours. It was a utopia. Each red, green and blue intertwined and danced, the perfect partners in a dance of beauty and light. And a gentle fog would fall upon the grounds, yet no ghoul or dark entity would appear. Instead the crystal buildings and stunning glows would illuminate the shadows. Even death itself, found glory and beauty within the kingdom, refusing to take the inhabitants to the next life. Life was born in this place. A place of peace and joy. This dance of emotion, contorted and manipulated vigorously to adapt and change… and when the dawn of a new day graced the courtyard, all the families, children, men and women were in unity. Love was born. You see, John… madness is deceptive and cunning. You would not hear, see or taste it yet behind your eyes it watches. Trust you will choose the right path… the path that will lead you to the Kingdom of Glass."

The night was longing, Caladrius had long since gone back to his silent solitude and I was left staring at the flickering flame, as the unforgiving winters breeze slithered into the cave. I was unsure whether it was the cave itself or maybe the presence of the deity, that seemingly made my mind deviate into thoughts that I would never usually consider. My mind commonly could be found to be plagued with ideas that weren't mine. Ideas from my acquaintances of anxiety and sadness in the cave were hushed into no more than whispers. The thoughts that further prevailed seemed to be that of calmness and clarity. The thick fog that was absent from my vision yet tangible in my mind had begun to dissipate. The clarity was something that became somewhat addictive in my mind which swiftly became attached to the incessant dripping of the melted ice from the stalactites, the stale breathing from the man lodged in the wall and the cold that made sure the hairs on my back were always up. Despite the kind hospitality of Ichilla in the grand city of Amor Ceriel, and the smiles from the woman of Thornfief, this was the first time I felt I could belong in the wildlands.

I must've been in a slumber dreaming dreams which clearly held no place in my conscious, as I was awoken by the ramblings of Caladrius.

"Ah, finally awake! Looks like it will be an interesting morn for you, sir!" he said, not even peering down at me.

Looking towards the exit of the cave I could see that the once beautiful sunrise was tainted by a smear of black which rose into the clouds.

"Smoke? A fire?" I questioned.

"Smells like war. You better run."

My legs bolted down the hillside, stumbling over hills of snow, never did my knees feel so weak, yet forced to work. I could feel each breath more than I could see the vapours dissipate into the frosty air. The snowflakes that departed the skies were immediately melted by the warmth of my skin, red with fear and anxiety which hit me like a war-hammer, mid swing, the moment I stepped into the sunlight from the comfort of the cave. The air was course, each long inhale was followed by a swift exhale and an abrupt splutter. What was once a beautiful view overlooking the green of the country that was bathed in the warm suns glow and was now nothing more than silhouettes burdened with grey and white patches of snowfall. The chaos of the snow, of the sharp winds and the burning skies was little, when inside my head a chaos was brewing that dimmed the external battle with the cold harshness of nature. A concoction of anxieties manifested and began to feast on the ideas carefully placing a sly poison in the smallest and most intricate parts of my mind. Caladrius had to be misled. The wars of the wildlands had always been raged on the oak tree whose roots strangled the stray sheep, or the beast who persisted on scraping its blood-soaked talons on the great gates of Amor Ceriel. Never would kings or noblemen attack one another, especially after the horrors of the civil war that left a scar across all the villages of the wildlands.

Amor Ceriel, the great city of the wildlands, known for its nobility and prestige, was now beaten and had been degraded to become a manifestation of the most potent of all human instincts… survival. Upon returning into the city where I had first laid eyes on the whispering throne, the stench of desperation filled the air, a strong un-mistakable scent. Helms of battle were being placed on the heads of young fair-haired boys, as they lugged swords half their size behind them trailing in the mud. Prospectors and priests stood tall in view of many, preaching to crowds of how the world would become engulfed in flame, consumed by the eternal fires fuelled by curses, forged from the sins of man. Order had become nothing more than a word, scurrying like ants, the people fled from door to door and the screams of the few amplified by the tears of the many. Forcing open the doors to the halls again and the whispers from the throne once again reached my ears – my fragile ears.

"Mes uroj dahya irlai."

The thrones mutterings were irresistible and as it spoke the distant screams reached an eerie silence.

"John!" a familiar voice echoed, breaking my focus from the trap of the Whispering Throne.

Ichilla confidently paced down the steps with his arms outstretched. I was unsure if he was expecting an embrace among friends?

"I suppose you must be wondering what might be happening here then, eh?"

"Explain, Ichilla," I demanded.

He continued to flaunt towards me before wrapping his arm around me, as he had done before.

"Nothing for you to worry about, my hero. Quite simply, I… We have had a slight disagreement with the neighbouring villages."

"Which ones?" I queried, with every intention that hopefully my knowledge of the wildlands would serve me well.

"All of them. Burncorn, Thornfief and Freshwater; but listen, its nothing for you to worry about."

He firmly gripped my shoulders looking at me with the eyes of a desperate child.

"What do you want from me, Ichilla? Is my crusade to save this country not enough?"

"You will save the country. More importantly, you will save Amor Ceriel. All from the misled people and noblemen of the villages. Prepare for war."

Deep in thought, I became unusually aware of my heartbeat, each pulse a thudding boom that shook my entire body. A wandering mind is the most dangerous one. Absent from where I was or the events that transpired in front of my eyes, I was left scanning through memories. 'Prepare for war' was a phrase I feared, the implications shattering all potential ideas for my future or the idea of return to my homeland.

"John? John you there?"

I picked my eyes up from the floor of my room to see Ichilla standing a few steps from me approaching me with caution.

"I suppose you have a few questions."

"Ichilla, what're you doing? This was not anything we had planned. My purpose was not for war... not with the people whom I am supposed to be saving!"

"No, no, this is where you're wrong, John," Ichilla said rising towards me, with such aggression. "You; you agreed to save this country and to save the wildlands. No matter what it entailed," he argued.

"Not to wage war on my neighbours!" I said, feeling small beads of tears forming in my eyes and a lump in my throat.

I was afraid. Afraid of the war, afraid of the land, afraid of what Caladrius would say. Most prominently, at this moment in time I was afraid of Ichilla. The fair-haired man sat next to me, embracing me how a father would.

"I promise we will see the dawn of a new day that we created John. Me and you, the architects of peace for a new world. This war… It's a steppingstone. A thread in a quilt. It's okay, John… It's okay."

His voice, softer this time, bringing tears from my eyes as he continued to wrap his arms around my shoulders. I had to trust Ichilla. He was my friend. We were on this journey together – a pairing that would be heroes to a new world.

Chapter 13

Casting the First Stone – The Battle of the Field of Emeralds

"I… I didn't know… at first I refused to believe it. I thought it was just a dream, an illusion. I always conspired that the Throne would take its toll on me. The constant whispers and mutterings; after a while it becomes rhythmic. Like a song. A tune of an unknown language, with notes that are yet to fall on human ears. I remember the pale look on the face of my fellow soldier as he burdened me with the news of the villages. You've seen the path they're on, John. You've seen the monster that is, Sir Nash and how he treats Burncorn. You've seen the corrupt nature of Freshwater. They are becoming animalistic and dangerous. They… they took my love from me. I don't expect you to completely understand my reasoning, John. But we need a shift in power."

Ichilla seemed different as he spoke – sadness with a touch of sincerity. I never knew what it was like to lose someone. I couldn't begin to believe the pain Ichilla felt upon learning of the savages who took the life of someone he loved. Did it really justify war? Maybe when he previously mentioned war, he meant a small battle, nothing like the civil war from years prior. It couldn't be. But whether I liked it or not, this was something I had to do in order to follow my path.

"Ichilla… if this war will bring about the change in the wildlands that we yearn for, then so be it. Let's go to war."

"Thank you, John… really, thank you," he said, standing and walking towards the door, brushing his hair back behind his ears. "I want you to go to the barracks. Meet all the knights. We march towards Burncorn tomorrow when the sun is tall."

And now I was only a day away from being in my first war. To find the barracks you only had to follow the smell of ale and the clashing of steel. The barracks were located just a few paces outside the keep presumably for Ichilla's safety. I could see how Ichilla could be misconstrued negatively and make enemies and evidently, he was just as aware, being wise enough to place soldiers' steps from his bed. I was not shocked to see that I seemed to be the smaller of most of the soldiers as they towered over me, built like giants and bred for war. I approached the small tent with caution, my eyes curiously wondering over to the table on which sat maps and tactical documents of sorts.

"Ello, fella," a rather tall man said, turning to face me.

His starved face and slender build was certainly not what I had envisioned for a soldier of the most prestigious army in the wildlands. By the shock on his face I gathered that I was not the 'hero of the plains' that he had hoped for.

"You lost?" he spoke again.

His words were very pronounced – his mouth dextrous wrapping around each vowel and syllable.

"No, I ermm… Ichilla told me to come here. My name's John."

"Ahh, that Sawyer lad? Heard you butchered that snare in Thornfief!"

My frail mortality was still in flux about the recent events especially the madness that consumed me – the same madness that killed the snare. I remained silent giving a vague shrug.

"Ahh, word travels fast you see. You'll likely be able to slay a few Burncornians tomorrow then?"

"Ignore him… if he makes you feel uncomfortable," a separate bolder voice emanated from a different room.

However, the voice was just as prominent. The voice was given a face, as in walked a lady. Again, she was tall, just taller than I, her short brunette hair was rare for a woman. However, being in the military, she too was bred for combat.

"Ignore me? Surely not. I'm the life of the party, love. The names Speak."

"You're an arse, Speak and if you dare refer to war as a 'party' again I will gut you," she muttered inches from Speak's face, with each vowel she spat a little with some landing on the blade she held towards his throat.

I was never the most intelligent person in the room; however, it didn't take a genius to see that the woman wasn't to be trifled with and if I were to survive the encounter, I had to muster up every ounce of respect I could.

"You must be the fresh one…" She exclaimed in my direction raising her voice as did her expectations.

"Yes, my name is…"

"Oh, I know who you are. Slayer of the snare. That little scuffle won't make the enemy hesitate as they swing their sword at the weak points in your armour." She scowled, her eyes sharper than her knife, which had yet to be sheathed as she left the tent.

"Don't worry 'bout her. She's always like this. Specially cause we going to war tomorrow," Speak said, putting his hand on my shoulder, directing me out to the courtyard while my attention was still captured by the woman who had just shouted at me.

"How long have you been a knight?" I enquired to the taller man as he admired a rack of swords, choosing carefully which one he would take to battle.

"Not long enough to know the colour of blood, my friend."

"That doesn't instil confidence," I said, as Speak began to swing his chosen blade around, whirling and twirling it.

He seemed to be a sorcerer with a blade.

"But Amor Ceriel was a city practically made for war. Years ago, back before the land took its first breath, there were the First Company. The first 13 beings to ever set foot on the land. Ya know, I've only ever heard stories and rumours but apparently, they could carve the mountains with their fingertips. They could command the seas and the sun would only rise if they permitted it. But of course, they were still only human. One of the First Company butchered the others. No one knows why. They all fell, their blood spilling on the land, breathing life into it. The land was gifted colour, the trees began to sway and the rain fell upon a living land. Then the last being of the First Company gave his life to birth humans… then the first humans built Amor Ceriel. See, the city has been standing for centuries by a being bred for war. Now, it won't fall, John. Not to a few Burncornians."

That night, when the moon was basking in the blackness of a mid-autumn sky, a silence fell upon Amor Ceriel. Many houses in the lower city were full of families gathered around a loved one, a man who would soon be another soldier to march into the abyss of chaos. If you looked over the city from one of the many spires, no lights would be seen, however you might just hear the grinding of stone on a blade as they are prepped to taste the blood of the neighbouring villages. It was up on one of these spires I stumbled across the woman from the tent.

"Oh, I'm sorry, I didn't know you were up here."

I began to scurry back down the stairs, expecting a hurl of vulgar words to follow me.

"We go to war tomorrow, John. I know of your battle with the snare. Do you have what it takes to kill a man?"

"I… I just want to do the right thing. Ichilla said I was going to drain the darkness from this land. That together we would cleanse it."

"A hero himself among my ranks… we can't lose then," she said with a great impulse of sarcasm, even making herself grin a feat which I thought impossible.

"I wish you a bloody battle and if death arrives on that battlefield, I wish you a swift journey to the next life."

And with those words, she disappeared down the stairway of the spire, leaving me looking over the dark emptiness of Amor Ceriel, the great city on its last night of peace.

The cold was bitter as was the silence that continued to haunt the city throughout the night. Stars littered the sky, only to soon be diminished by passing clouds driven by unseen strong winds that battered the skies and equally the lands. Doors of houses rattled on their rusting hinges and the occasional quiet shriek of a rodent echoed around the columns of the maze of architecture. The underlying tone of the drumming of war silently built throughout the city.

When the moon fell and the sun took its place, I was still hesitant to leave the bed I was in. The night didn't bring me sleep and I doubted I was the only one to have not visited their subconscious. Instead the night consisted of being in an apotheosis of sweating, nail biting and the endless feeling of a sinking heart. Daylight didn't dispel the feeling, with it still being prominent even as I clothed myself, sat on the bed transfixed by my sword and the chainmail given to me by Speak before I was a soldier. Back when I was a man. Surely this couldn't be happening. Ever since arriving in this country I felt a fog descend not over my eyes but a thick layer clouded my mind. It was as if the last few days had simply been a nightmare – a reality that wasn't true. And now I was due to be marching upon Burncorn before the sun reached the height of the skies. My mind pondered over the inscription still perceivable on my blade. The blade that had never tasted the blood of a man before. Hell, it hadn't even tasted blood at all! And now it was going to be held in the hands of a man who is too afraid to wield it. A knock arrived at my door, one that I had been dreading all night and all morning. The door cracked open and Speak pushed his head through.

"Morning, sunshine!"

His words did not elicit a response from me, so he took to sitting beside me on the bed.

"Nervous?" I enquired, expecting another few words of sarcasm or a joke to do with Ichilla being too short to go to war.

"… Sleepless night of tears… you?"

"Yeah… I didn't come here expecting war," I said.

"No one expects war. Justified or not. But this is one that we must partake in for the betterment of Amor Ceriel."

"Of course. I guess."

"Let's go… captain will be expecting us."

He stood and made his way to the door, leaving a few words before going to the courtyard. "If I die, John, I'm glad I met the man who's going to change the fate of the wildlands."

That day, the grass looked dim. As if the colour had left it in preparation of what was to come. Everyone was silent. All thousand men, pale as ghosts, sweating litres. All thousand men confined to silence by their fear – the only thing making them walk towards death was their pride. The marching had become rhythmic and almost hypnotising. The armour I brandished was heavy and on occasion locked at the joints. The helmet meant it was a task just to see and the sound of my breathing became amplified, the raspy irregular breaths that became shorter and tighter until they became nothing more than a sharp inhale. Pins stabbed at my fingers, which was the only sign I could tell they were there, for the rest of my arms felt numb. This made me ponder whether I was going to be able to draw my sword at all, let alone swing it against another suit of armour. The ninth battalion held no other man I knew; I wondered where Speak was, perhaps with the captain. Soon the unsettling noise became apparent to our ears. The rhythm of our haste, the patterned sound of our marching was mirrored but different. Just over the hill, we arrived at the Field of Emeralds. It was named the Field of Emeralds due to the depth of the green velvet grass that scattered itself over the area. However, the famed coloured grass refused to show on this day leaving a dull green, which if I didn't know better could've been an even more dull grey. The marching stopped as we came to a halt on the hill, listening intently to the rustling of armour and the unmistakable noise of steel leaving its sheathe. Peering over the shoulder of the slightly taller gent in front of me, I could see the enemy lines. The army of Amor Ceriel was noticeably larger; however, this didn't diminish the feeling of nausea that was brewing in my stomach. Then from the silence grew shouts – the shouts of desperate men. The primal shouts, screams and cries of war. The physical manifestation of the purest form of human instinct being shown on the battlefield moments before blood being spilt… survival. The unity of the shouts of war encouraged my frail anxiety-riddled body to shout too, with tears streaming down my cheeks. And then, began the charge. My legs moved as quick as I could move them, the clunking of steel pulling me down. By the time I had reached the bottom of the hill, where the grass was supposed to be greener, the breath had left my lungs and air seemed to become even more scarce. The clash of steel and the pungent smell of iron filled the air, the spray of blood painted the pristine steel armour that housed the precious fleshy bodies of afraid men. The suits of armours swung at anything that moved, anything that cried or screamed. Afraid, I kept moving, yet to swing my sword at all. Until the dreaded fear became reality as I spied another suit of armour and they too spied me. I knew we were both thinking the same thing, just two men scared to make the first move, scared to spill the blood of another man. As I took a step, so did he and we knew what was going to happen. Our swords clashed, the jolt of the impact travelling up my arm aching my shoulders. Again, we swung and I began to question if we were both aiming for the sword of the other to prolong the battle and reduce the amount of blood on our hands. Swing after swing, shout and squeal, the fight went on, until time took its course and I landed a clean slash down upon the shoulder of the enemy suit. Our reckless scuffle came to an end, the suit calmly dropped his weapon. Reaching up and removing his helm I saw a boy reaching the end of childhood. Spitting blood on the floor, tears in his eyes, without a loved one on his deathbed. And death claimed its first victim from my hands. Before the boy's body went cold, another sword swing came from the left, narrowly missing my head. This suit was slightly larger and I could envision little remorse on the face of this man. His strikes felt different, the unrivalled power to any I had felt before. Questionably unparalleled even to the snare. Fear consumed my being; a sinking feeling rose that congealed my blood and seized my arms as strike after strike the man ruthlessly persisted. Until a new, yet familiar feeling from the back of my mind came forward, a feeling I despised yet welcomed hesitantly. Sanity once again left my body; a deep unawakened madness took the reins of the armour and more dangerously… the sword. A fast flurry of short sharp strikes from my sword changed the tides of the fight as the man in armour rose his sword high to protect himself. I found myself screaming and shouting manically as each swing further depleted the defence of the enemy. Until my body did the unpredictable. Unable to react I threw down my sword despite every thought telling me to stop and proceeded to leap at the man, tackling him to the floor and repeatedly planted my hand on his face. Like an ape, I smashed his helmet like glass, so his skull was unimaginably easy to follow. Like a beast I ripped my helm from my head and used it to pulverise the remaining fragments of bone that lay in the remains of his helmet. Before spying another 'victim' which I ran at and it met a similar fate. I forced him to the ground before ripping his helmet from his head and with just three punches he no longer breathed or cried. But the ounce of sanity that remained inside surfaced as the face was one I knew. A friendly face. The kind face of a farmer. The face of a Burncornian.

"Y… yen?" I muttered, as all my tears shed.

Chapter 14
The Friendly Hand

The never-ending shakes of dread. Scars of the recent events, planting me firmly in the past, unable to move on. Yen's face was a kind one, one that was still very fresh in my memory despite it being months since we last met. The tainted memory of his face. The blood spilling from his nose, eyes, mouth and ears and feeding into the Field of Emeralds. The shakes never end. A constant jitter in the hands, as if they have an awareness. An awareness that I'm afraid. They aren't wrong. The march back to Amor Ceriel was painful. In the physical sense, my body ached. Each joint had seized up, making movement a painful experience even without armour. The emotional distress had become a burden to bear. The piles of bodies had built up in my conscience. Sat in the tent, the barracks filled with the joy of victory. I saw it as anything but, there cannot be victory in war, for either side. Yen the good farmer was dead, his blood forever staining my hands. I killed a young boy, stealing his life from him without question. In silence I waited, for the inevitable. The 'victorious' soldiers stood to attention called by the woman who, rather than basking in victory, seemed anxious. A familiar man sat opposite me. He shared not my loss, but he still dared not look me in the eyes, possibly out of respect of a tormented soldier.

"John? You're alive…"

Still I sat in silence. The words of Ichilla barely reached my ears.

"Burncorn has been defeated. Their whole village lay in ruins. Sir Nash lay dead in the soil. John they will re-build under my… our rule. Imagine the utopia it will become? The second great city of the wildlands."

I pondered on the idea of the great city it may become. One similar to Amor Ceriel no doubt, with spires reaching for the clouds – a city of beauty and safety. However, it will not be a city of dreams. It will be no Kingdom of Glass.

"It will be a city built on the corpses of those who founded it," I said, too afraid to look Ichilla in the eyes.

His stare of detest weighed heavy on me, unknowingly.

"John… don't question what you did. In order to craft a chair, a tree must first be culled. The vision I see John…"

"Does your vision account for the death of the many?" I felt him retract from the conversation, folding his arms and sitting back out from my peripheral.

He took a moment before saying, "I feel each death… every person slew by the swords of my men is never forgotten. John, we can fix this. This is the first step in our new world."

My silence beckoned him away, with a gentle friendly pat on my shoulder he was gone. The silence became infectious.

The buzz of victory wore thin – each of the soldier's morale dropping like flies. One by one they became consumed by the harrowing afterimage of war. The ones of death held a tight grip on those who murdered them. That night enough tears were cried to fill a lake. Each and every man fallen into

114

the abyss. Their morality lay askew with no direction. The black and white intertwined into a very questionable grey, as each of them wrestle with their conscience. That night was the second night sleep left me. I lay, forced to live in a reality where my actions were screaming and banishing me from sleep. Nightmares had broken from my subconscious and had manifested in front of my eyes, the vision of the battered and broken bodies slain in battle never leaving my eyes. My eyes that lost their innocence the moment I thrusted the blade into that young man's shoulder. A separate sense of rationality argued with the other voices in my head that accused me. 'Murderer', they called me, the crime that cannot be forgiven for the forgiver is dead. I'm stuck pulling at my hair – a thick layer of sweat seething from my forehead. Tears persistently streaming from my bloodshot eyes and the cries of post war.

Terragoth had become a second home to me now, the visits becoming more frequent. Caladrius was consistently there, offering a sense of routine and confidence. The incredible intelligence he possessed made him more than just a friend. While I was in bed breaking down, the simple but powerful thought etched into my brain. The idea that Caladrius would know of the madness that abducted sanity from me on the battlefield. The same madness that consumed me that night of the blood moon. The journey became easier, my singular footprints eventually became an eroded path in the snow, one I could follow with certainty that it would lead me to the place I needed to be. Every time I stepped foot in that cave and heard the dripping of melting stalactites I was filled with a familiar sense of peace.

"Caladrius?" I said cautiously entering the depths of the cave.

"Always here, aren't I?" a voice said, the voice of a wise old man stuck in the walls of the cave.

"I feel like I'm owed some answers," I demanded, timidly.

"Hm. And some answers you are owed. Some you are not ready to hear yet."

I took a few seconds to compose myself, shuffling the words of the explanation around in my head to make an efficient sentence.

"I… I keep losing myself. Especially in war."

"Ahh right… I know what you're talking about. You see, you may not be the only one, John, but if it's an explanation you want then I'm happy to give one. Though it may be a disappointment to you. The First Company?"

I felt a sense of relief that I had some sort of idea of what Caladrius was speaking of.

"Yes, yes I've heard about them."

"The First Company were the first beings on the wildlands. Like deities they were. Not gods but still mighty for the first people to walk these parts. Thirteen of them there was. And they lived in peace for the longest time, long even before I was put in this bloody rock. But, as I'm sure you know, one of them killed the other twelve."

"Yeah, that's right. That's what Speak said."

Could Caladrius simply be reciting the story of the First Company? How could that explain my question? Caladrius tilted his head, sensing I was in thought.

"Then the murderer of the twelve gave his life to create the first humans who built Amor Ceriel and were the architects of the foundations of the country. Well, lemme tell you something, kid, something that not many people know.

The survivor of the First Company? The one who murdered his twelve brothers and sisters? His name… was Madness."

There was truly little shock that came with the words of Caladrius. The identity of the murderer of the twelve couldn't be the reasoning for the problems I had encountered.

"I know it's unlikely that the name will be much help to you now, but all will become clear."

"When, Caladrius? When will it become clear? I'm just so confused, and… and ever since arriving here, it's just been one big riddle, a secret that has been hidden from me. First the nonsense with Cassandra Boyle and now I've become a soldier in a war that I didn't want."

I couldn't resist the impulse of aggression that was anchoring its way into my tone of voice. I knew why I felt the way I did. I knew why the aggression was presenting itself in such a way. I was afraid. Afraid of everything in this place. I was afraid, for being thrown onto a path of which I didn't know the destination. An unsure path that, I too was unsure I could follow. I was certain Caladrius had made a mistake. That Ichilla found the wrong man – I couldn't be the saviour he was searching for. My mind grew tiresome from the games of the powers and elites. The unknown destination of the journey I was thrust into invented a deep worry that continued to grow inside. Each time I climbed the snowy cliffs of Terragoth, I always expected the crusty aged lips of Caladrius to form the words, 'This is the end.' I was firmly aware that he knew how this story would end. But time is a relentless and merciless force. I had no choice but to kneel and bow my head as I took part in a game of lies and war, to follow a path I knew nothing of. The man in the wall sighed deeply and I knew the sigh had words etched into the helpless, wasted breath.

"The time isn't right… is it?" I said with disappointment.

"The madness, John… look for it, riddled within you. And when it bares its fangs again be ready. Keep your sanity."

The city of Amor Ceriel was united through war. War brought the people together in a way that no method of peace could. Now knowing of the role of madness in everyone, I could see how people were comfortable in war. No longer did they cry and shake with the fear of finance or starvation. Instead they revelled in the chaos of war. I sat by the fountain in the city and watched as the sun from an endless day was put to rest behind the great spires of the first city of the wildlands. The words of Caladrius never really left my ears, his wise voice echoed endlessly as I pondered over the deeper meaning of his riddles.

The victory at the field of emeralds was still fresh in the minds of the joyous citizens who praised their soldiers and knights. The knights who humbly yet reluctantly accepted the praise, while stewing in their memories were the wicked actions of war. Ichilla bathed in the glory. It wasn't till the evening that a steward arrived at my dorm, knocking gently on the glossed wooden door before inviting me to a party, a gathering of sorts. Despite the slight anxiety of conversation, I could hardly decline the offer after fighting in a war. I searched the room with haste, questioning myself of the attire I could wear. I was never one to appear fashionable. For me, clothing was to be functional and that was always the goal when I wore clothing. Could it keep me warm? Could I run in it? Could I move enough in it if I were to fight or climb? Pointless questions perhaps but to me this was more important than if a certain lacing or seam looked appealing. I saw a tunic, a green swirling pattern sown into the fabric, the colour dull yet with a brighter green laced throughout the material. Hesitantly I lifted it from the wardrobe and to my surprise it was almost as straining as lifting chainmail. I was shocked at how thick the material was.

"Aw crap... this can't be..." I muttered before turning to see the steward still at the door, horrified at my musings of the tunic.

"It's pretty... really... really pretty," I said, however the disapproved look in his eyes showed that he'd heard enough, before leaving abruptly without saying a word.

I prayed he never said a word to Ichilla. I didn't want to appear disrespectful. Putting on the tunic was the hardest task I had yet faced. The rigid material refused to shift, like bark it was stiff, which made it tasking to fit over my head. Immediately a hot sweat seared on my forehead. I couldn't tell if it was due to the calamity of the tunic or the sight of hundreds of people dressed similar to me, all of them appearing in their comfort zone... and not sweating. The floor felt wobbly and unstable and my knees almost buckling with each step.

"John? How are you doing?" a voice sounded.

I saw the woman from the front lines. The captain, the commander of the leading knight garrison. She bore a similar tunic, vastly different from her rugged battle dress. I had never noticed the colour of her eyes before. Not a pale blue, but a deep wise blue, giving a certain 'thickness' to the colour. As I considered this, I noticed I was yet to respond to her question, her look of kindness gradually changing to one of concern.

"Yeah, yeah, no, yes I am well, I'm good. I didn't expect you here?"

"Are you disappointed?" A noticeable playfulness became apparent.

"No, no, not at all!"

"Of course, I went to war too John. I am surprised you made it out! We share this victory."

Her smile was one that seemed so familiar. Never had I seen her smile. It was one that glowed, complimenting her kind gentle eyes. I spent the evening sat in the garden, the wonderful garden that Ichilla first introduced me to that fateful day. Joining me, sat on the marble bench, was the commander, the woman with the deep blue eyes. She told me of how she arrived in this land as a child. A child brought to the wildlands, the land which breathed. How dangerous it would be to bring up a child in the depths of the alive lands. She fought for Ichilla for years, his army becoming a part of her, an extension of her personality. The woman had defended Amor Ceriel for years, her deep blue eyes seeing more blood than I could possibly comprehend. When she told me this, silence overcame her and she was absolved in thought. I contemplated; *was she feeling guilty? Fearful?*

"How many stars do you think there are, John?" she asked with sincerity.

"One for every breath of a new-born child. Enough to have a new shining pinprick of light for every thought I could have about this place, the wildlands, Amor Ceriel and you."

She gave a slight chuckle coupled with a sigh. Her valuable gaze still fixed on the sky. The sky was deep like her eyes, a darkness unlike any other I had seen since my arrival. This darkness was calm and beautiful. And she gazed into the endless night, the clusters of stars thrown into the sky. A mess of chaotic order, but a simple beauty could be found in the irregular patterns of stars that dotted the black skies, not plagued with clouds.

"Don't think I haven't realised," she said; in doing so a sharp fear hit me, far more than what was needed. "You never even asked my name."

Well aware that I in fact had never asked for her name I responded, "Haven't I? That's strange?"

She giggled again. "My name is Estrilda. It's nice to meet you, stranger from a faraway land. Saviour of Amor Ceriel."

"Nice to meet you, Estrilda of the Leading Garrison of Amor Ceriel."

Chapter 15

The Beast of Dreams

The night of the party was enjoyment sure, however I certainly felt my place was not to become a host of sorts for others enjoyment. I simply searched for the end of this war and the forthcoming of a new world. The burning sun rose again, and I awakened, not in a state of panic or fear but once I woke in peace. My subconscious mind wondered in my sleep, bringing forth images of Estrilda, Speak and my old life back home. The odd amalgamation of the lives I have lived entwined into a life in which I could finally rest and smile without madness and fear. I awoke with the thoughts still brimming in my mind, before halting with the realisation that it was a dream and the life I dreamt was fictitious. After clothing myself in the fresh silk that was provided to me by Ichilla, I marched down to the hall still contemplating the thoughts of the dream. Gradually more thoughts seeped through the cracks, of the war, Ichilla and Caladrius.

"Hello, stranger! Nice of you to show yer face," a familiar voice said.

"Speak! I haven't seen you since Emerald Fields. I thought you dead," I said, wrapping my arms around him.

The battle had become a mere blur in my mind and only the sharp images of the death I had caused remained.

"Takes more than a few sods with swords to off me. I plan to take over when Ichilla kicks the bucket," he said with a smirk, leering to the King of Amor Ceriel who looked upon him, unamused.

"What're you doing here?" I asked.

Usually only Ichilla would sit upon his Whispering Throne during the early sun rise.

"Dunno, the blond called us here."

Ichilla rose from the Throne, sincerity masking his usual smiling face. "Yes... I asked you three here. The Throne has been telling me of things; such... terrible things. A man bleeding from his eyes. A woman weeping over a burning flower. And a boy, speaking of a beast in his head... a beast that concerns even the might of the Whispering Throne. I want you to go to the boy. Find what's happening."

"But, lord, the war?" Estrilda said, reverting back to the persona of the war general, a persona I didn't connect with as much as the Estrilda I met before at the party.

"I am aware of the war. Of course, I am aware of the war, General, it's my city. How can we fight to save a city from man, if a beast too is present in the wildlands? One foe is enough; wouldn't you agree?"

"Yes... yes, Lord."

Estrilda paced out from the halls, with Speak silently following her, like any soldier would for their general. I followed until the commanding voice of Ichilla caught up with me.

"John, a word please."

"Of course," I said, hiding a sigh and greeting him with a friendly smile.

"John, listen… I care about you. I care about Estrilda. You have to understand…" he said placing his hand on my shoulder as he had done countless times before. "I only want what's best for my city. For the wildlands. They are misguided John. Even the likes of Estrilda and Speak wouldn't understand. They are following their hearts. They will hold back the problems, using all their power to try and stop the onslaught. The onslaught is coming, John; the only way it can be stopped is with you. On that note…"

A cloud of darkness overcame the conversation as Ichilla took a moment to collect himself.

"This, boy… I trust you will do the right thing should the situation arise."

I was never the most intelligent man, nor was I innately perceptive but even I understood the implications of Ichilla's words. I gave a faint hollow nod before turning away from him. As I left the hall, I felt his gaze on me as the whispers of the Throne slowly got lost in the echoes of the chamber. Outside I found the other members of the party waiting for me with impatience.

"Ichilla scares me sometimes…" Speak said as I approached.

Estrilda muttered, "Where do we start? We know nothing of this boy. Where he is? Not even a name?"

I lacked knowledge of the wildlands so I was aware that I would be of no help at this point in the expedition. However, I did know one being who was capable of finding the boy.

"I know how…" I said knowing the next few sentences in the conversation wouldn't be in the favour of Speak and especially Estrilda.

"How?" she queried.

"More like who," I said.

"Okay, then who?"

"Tirynn of Freshwater."

Tirynn was a liar and a cheat. But his ability to walk among the endless streams of the astral plane made him a useful asset. The day was grim. A dull sky with clouds that dripped leaving a passer-by in constant state of wonder if rain were to cascade upon the land or not. It almost seemed impossible that the grass could become even more dense, yet seemingly it was thicker and longer than the last time I ventured out among the wildlands.

In-between the pants and inhales of Speak, he found the air to say, "Do you know, John, The Field of Emeralds. I… I was so afraid, and after, boy, you don't understand how much I felt valued. The gods must be looking upon us, right? That feeling of bliss didn't last long though. It ended when Ichilla told me what all the villages of the wildlands had renamed it. The Field of Rubies. Where the once deep green grass is now drowning in the blood of martyrs."

Speaks voice cracked as the memories overcame him, a strong supressed sadness surfaced and sent Speak into a silence full of repent and regret. He walked a few steps ahead, taking a moment to compose himself. Now wasn't the time for tears.

"Death affects people in different ways, John…" Estrilda spoke up from behind me.

"Yeah. I remember before the battle. Speak was so different."

"Becoming numb to death is the hardest part of war. Amor Ceriel has suffered more deaths in the aftermath of war than during the act itself."

"Yen… he was the first person I met in this country. He was kind. His hospitality was unrivalled. Sometimes he didn't come across as the nicest man. More times than not I felt disliked by him – I even convinced myself that I was a burden to him. But in the end, when he shook my hand, his wise eyes spoke more about him than anyone else possibly could. During the battle… my first ever war, the armour felt heavy and the ground kept shaking beneath my feet. My sword never cut through the air so slow. I killed Yen… with my own hands, I shattered him to pieces."

Without uttering a word, Estrilda hugged me; the tears in her eyes saying all that needed to be said. I felt another pair of arms as Speak too embraced us. The effects of war like a plague spread through all the ranks of the soldiers, even to Speak, Estrilda and myself. Marching to war, you fear death. After war, when what remains of your army shout and hands raise in victory, you feel a sense of relief and of safety. However, no one seemed to understand. There is no victory in war. The trauma lay dormant, haunted just behind the eyes of each witness of war, lingering ready to smite.

Thunder cracked and storms raged as us three cloaked figures stumbled through dirt and mud. Our trajectory pointed at Freshwater. A place where we were outcasts and enemies. Deemed as threat to their village, which was slowly crumbling under the pressure of the growing empire of Amor Ceriel. They didn't seem to understand that their defeat would bring

126

a new start for them, free from the sinister on looking shadow of the wildlands. Through the merciless hordes of rain from the strikes of lightning that briefly illuminated the fields before us, the remote village of Freshwater was in sight. And with our steps aimed towards the village, the daunting journey to find Tirynn was to be concluded. The old gates of Freshwater were swinging on their hinges with each gentle blow of the wind a distinct creak would sound with the bellowing undertone of the storm. With caution we entered. Speak insisted on entering first – he mocked the inferior village making a remark on how they couldn't even keep out a pack of wolves. The damp fog from the plains had somehow dispersed in the city changing into a thick smoke which wore at the weary eyes of us three travellers from Amor Ceriel. The once peaceful town, with artistic architecture had become absolved by riots. Mothers abandoned their children to run riot, howling about the end of times. Men drank and bottles smashed.

"Keep your eyes down... we move swiftly," Estrilda said, giving me a forceful push into the heart of the village.

I dreaded to comprehend what they would do should they find out we hail from the city of war. The drought of sanity was evident in this place and I was burdened to keep the silence on the sudden realisation that these people had encountered madness, just as I had. I felt the ever-watching eyes of Caladrius. I knew he would've wanted me to see this, a warning, showing me what I could become should I lose the ongoing internal warfare, the raging battle as my sanity held on by a thread. These internal thoughts must've been externalised to some extent as a touch on my shoulder followed by the words of Speak.

"John? You still with us?"

I clicked back to reality, noticing that my gaze was fixed upon a burning house.

"Yeah… yeah I'm okay… Tirynn isn't far. Just past the fountain."

"You sure you're all right, bud?" Speak said, his slender artistic hands gripping my arm, guiding me forward.

"I'm fine," I replied.

The house of Tirynn seemed untouched and vandals seemed to flee from it shouting, "Its him! The nightmare man!"

It was these comments that fed my suspicion. Could Tirynn be responsible for the beast trapped in the boys' mind? I thought this suspicion would justify the lack of knocking, as Speak kicked down the door and Estrilda and myself rushed the house. It seemed to be as I remembered all those months ago. The bones still on the floor and the trinkets and talisman still suspended from the ceiling. However, unlike last time, light was absent from the place.

"Ahh well, would you err see who decided to show up!"

Tirynn entered from the small cabinet room.

"Hello, nightmare man," I said, slyly inching past Estrilda who gripped the hilt of her blade.

"Hahahaha." Tirynn laughed feverishly, without consideration to my words.

Burping and slurping he mumbled, "Bloody hell, John, I been watching ya you know. Pretty ballsy to show up here again. Why don't you bloody go back to yer castles and spires and shit."

As he poorly delivered those lines, he pointed his crooked finger at me gripping a bottle of rum and swaying as if a strong wind were present in the room. Speak, appearing speechless, managed to question, "This is the man you suggested to help us? May as well just look for the kid ourselves."

"Yeah, you do that, pal." Tirynn giggled, causing Speak to lose his passive nature at that moment, punching the drunk man to the floor.

"Speak!" Estrilda reprimanded.

"Let John talk to him."

I crouched down, low enough that the smell of the alcohol on Tirynn's breath was stronger than the smoke in the surrounding area.

"What happened to you, Tirynn?"

The endearment in my voice sparked a reaction from the drunkard, who became tearful and apologetic. "I… I felt them all John… the battle at the Field of Emeralds. I felt them all die… they—they told us that it was the end. That the almighty power of Amor Ceriel dwarfed that of even the First Company. They told us to run and flee. That life had no value anymore. That us Freshwater folk were an embarrassment to the allied forces of the neighbouring villages. I… I…"

"It's okay… It's okay."

I knew how he was feeling. I could sense the depravity in him, an overwhelming sense of loss. The indoctrination of the people by their leader, all of them terrified because of the 'foreseen slaughter' at the hands of the army of Amor Ceriel. Tirynn's ability to walk the astral plane was always a mystery to me, a concept I couldn't quite grasp. However, I did know that the amount of blood that soaked the land at the Field of Rubies was enough to drive any man to insanity. Luckily, Tirynn found his salvation in the bottom of a bottle, numbing

the pain and holding back the imminent forces of madness…
or the rope from his neck.

"Tirynn, I need your help… Now more than ever okay?"
I spoke gently, as if speaking to a child.

Tirynn wiped his alcohol induced tears.

"What do you want, John?"

"We are looking for a child," Estrilda mentioned stepping
forward with her general's authority. I made the decision to
stay silent, as Estrilda took the lead. Confusing or further
upsetting Tirynn could've cost us.

"There are a lot of children in these villages woman."

A latent anger begun festering in the conversation
between the two.

"There is a boy we are searching for, drunk."

"Why? So, you can slaughter him too?" Tirynn uttered.

"You, shit…"

"Guys, come on…" I interrupted salvaging what I could
to save an alliance.

"We have a common enemy here. Despite the war
between Amor Ceriel and the neighbouring villages. And it
lay dormant in the mind of that boy. Please, Tirynn… find
him."

"I… know of the child you speak," Tirynn said with
reluctance.

"His name is Kolm. He rests in the remains of Burncorn.
The broken village. The fallen."

"And, what of the beast in his head?" Speak murmured.

Tirynn pulled at his hair before saying, "An infection. A
sort of fractured memory. A bleed. A nightmare that feasts on
the blood of dreams. Go to him. Should the nightmare escape
the mind of the boy… the world of man could fall."

The imminent departure of Freshwater was a welcome one. The dull ache of anxiety was left in the village as chaos fell upon the land like rainwater. I had a doubt that Ichilla knew of the effects that his war was having. Watching the fires burn the artistic architecture of Freshwater and seeing first-hand the water of the famed fountains boil. The sight was one that shook me, for it seemed most unnatural. Curiosity found its way into my thoughts, asking about William Thorn? He was a man for sure, however could the body of a child survive the madness that was infecting everyone? That was spreading at a rate that seemed implausible to the ears of a sane man? Estrilda remained quiet as we left and quieter still as we trudged through the wildlands on yet another trek to the broken village.

"John… I don't think I'm ready to go to Burncorn yet…" Speak uttered.

The absent look in his eyes was harrowing to one who remembered that the same eyes used to hold such joy. Guilt stained his conscience. Perhaps regret even. He didn't know of Ichilla's plan to reform the entirety of the wildlands justifying his scepticism.

"It's all right, Speak. It will be the same as Freshwater. Keep our eyes down and move fast."

I put my hand on his thin shoulders, his lanky frame shaking slightly. The cold was bitter, aiding the fear present with Speak. The sun fell tiresome as it painted the sky orange bringing the distinct white light of the pale moon flooding the country. The same moon that bled back when The Snare stalked the lands which felt like a lifetime ago.

The Whispers of the Throne became louder, even making their way into my dreams. They were subtle, so subtle I struggled to remember when they actually began. They may or may not have started when I saw the strands of saliva dripping from the jaws of Mr Brickenden back in the East Woods. The utterings may have started when I shook hands with Yen or after I splintered his skull. The more I thought about it, the more my mind ached. A dull ache, just behind the eyes, that became such an irritant I diverted my mind from the thoughts of the origin of the Whispers. But they were still there. Still present in my head whether they had my attention or not. Whenever Ichilla sat on his throne, twirling his blonde locks, scratching his beardless chin contemplating the future of his city, I knew he was listening intently to the Whispering Throne. I doubted he could possibly know that the Whispers weren't for his ears alone. I could sense the depth of each vowel. The pronunciation of each word articulated to be incoherent to our mortal ears. The immense weight of the syllables as they constructed words that were too advanced and ancient to comprehend. Carefully packaged into nothing more than almost silent mumblings that pained my mind as it attempted to deconstruct something that was never meant to be deconstructed. The deep waters I had been thrown into questioned all previous knowledge that I had convinced myself was true. The idea of the subconscious, the madness of which I feared immensely and the simple reality of survival. Materialism became obsolete. The trinkets I held, the sword I brandished or the clothes I wore became meaningless. Nothing else mattered, except survival. After the prophecy was announced to me through the gentle words of Ichilla, I knew that my destiny lied at the side of the King. Ruling a new world full of peace and wonder.

Apathy surfaced from the dormant mind of Speak, as he stepped over the debris that inhabited the corroded grounds of Burncorn. The lack of empathy wasn't in the nature of Speak, however it was the trauma that caused his disinterest in the situation. Retrieving the boy was his goal. Estrilda too seemed cold to the ruins of the city and refused to question the absence of people.

"Where is everyone?"

"Running… from war. Probably to Thornfief."

"You mean, running from us?" Estrilda's eyes spoke of defiance.

Disgusted that one of her 'soldiers' could suggest such a thing.

"Running from battle. A war is waged between two parties. Burncorn chose their fate," Speak said.

He didn't mean to be harsh. His words were simply an attempt to life some of the guilt from his conscience.

"They had no choice!" I argued. "And you? Did you? They had as much of a choice as you did… You picked up the sword, John," said Estrilda.

"Guys!" Speak interrupted, saving me from the verbal slaughter of Estrilda.

He gestured into the decrepit skeleton of an old house. The door was fractured and the windows incomplete with glass puzzled over the ground. Prying the door open triggered the webbing of arachnids to snap and the rats to scurry at the new predators that entered the room. The damp walls crumbled and the floorboards creaked, slightly denting with our footsteps. The room was the ghost of what used to be a family living space. The memories of children's laughter on a winter's morning were carried on the wind as it flowed through the remains of the building. Chairs were left untucked and the pots and pans cooking a mother's meal left to gather rot. A boy sat in the room surrounded by the toys that had lost their innocent vibrant colours.

"That's him?" Speak said, hesitant to approach the malnourished and pale child.

In these parts, approaching any figure alone in the dark could be a mistake. I knelt so my eyes levelled with the child, even though his eyes were tight shut.

"Hello... Are you Kolm?"

"No! No." The child whined. "I don't want a bath, please don't put me in the bath." He continued covering his ears.

"Kid's confused," said Speak.

"He's afraid," scolded Estrilda further closing the distance between her and the child with and outstretched hand. Her attention fully withdrawn into the closed eyes of the child so much so she didn't see the slight shadow that crawled up his arm.

"Estrilda!" I said grabbing her hand and pulling her from the immediate proximity of the child.

"What?" She aggressively hit my arm, which proceeded to throb.

"No, Estrilda... look," Speak said, his wide eyes seeming to shake, as they locked onto the shadow that continued to consume the youngster's body.

"Please I don't like the bath, don't give me a bath," he continued.

However, the words became infected by a rasp, a demonic undertone.

"I don't like baths, just please don't put me in the bath."

"Can I help yous?" a gritty voice mumbled from the side doorway.

The man responsible for the voice was short and not young by any means. His youth had left him long ago, leaving him with a hunched over and a cane acted as another leg. I could sense a heated rage projecting from Estrilda who took the opportunity to vent her aggression.

"What have you done to him?"

"I ain't done nothing, girl, pipe down."

The voice of this man was unheard of by my young ears, nor did Speak or Estrilda know of his origin and we dare not ask.

"E's a bloody Shell, int he?"

"T… then where's Kolm?"

"Well…"

Shells were common among the plains. Crafted from clay, absent from the light of day, a witchblood would slave away. Crafting a body that looked human, walked like a human and talked like a human. But they were made without a soul. The very thing that gave purpose and meaning, they did not have.

Chapter 16

The Beginning of Things

The Whispering Throne spoke of times when the sun was youthful before the times of man. Daylight stretched across the land for the first time and a woman squinted her eyes as they cautiously opened. She stood, an action that she had never taken part in before and she observed. A field with thick tall grass which she caressed with her gentle touch as she waltzed unknowingly. Her once sleeping eyes could finally awaken to the land of endless wonders which she had now found herself in. The rays of light photosynthesised and beamed through the skeletons of leaves in the summer's trees – luscious, rich, green leaves that, when a breeze blew, floated gracefully on the wind. These were the times when magic was not breathing fire or raising the dead, but simply the rising of the moon in the nights sky. These were the times before doubt crept into the minds of mortals and before any blood stained the lands. The woman continued to dance and bound with such beauty and ease among the green fields under the skies of cyan. However, to her surprise, she felt a pair of eyes watching her deep in the grass. She turned, not with fear or horror for those emotions hadn't been conceived yet.

"Hello?" she enquired.

"Hello, miss," a voice responded almost immediately as a young man stood from the cage of vegetation.

"Who are you?" the woman said with curiosity, still no negative thought entering the mind of the innocent.

"I could ask you the same thing!" the man said playfully, giving a smile.

"I'm not too sure… wait… yes, my name is Lapris."

The pauses in her sentence also gave the gent time to consider what his chosen name would be.

"Hmm…" he said. "Well, hello, Lapris. My name is Madness."

"Madness?" she iterated.

"Such a funny name for a strange man in a field."

"Y… yes I suppose," Madness replied with a nervousness that seamlessly faded into his vocabulary.

Lapris and Madness continued to stray across the fields, together unknowing of their origin and without questions. The beauty of their world had been ingrained in their minds and within their hearts, the twins had little reason to question. The sky was painted a fragrant blue, one that was appealing to the young eyes of Lapris. However, this made her swift to notice the imperfections, as a stream of black smoke cut through the blue purity.

"Madness, look! What is that? Can we speak with it? Why does it attack the sky?"

"I'm… I'm unsure. Let's get closer," Madness said, fuelled with curiosity as sparks ignited within him, and the two bounded for the ground beneath the black tainted sky.

The trees were fresh and the bark moist as it wrapped around trunks and branches. They seemed to refuse to line up, scattered in such a pattern that the tree line became a wall of wood and plantation that reached, coiled and constrained its way around everything within reach. However, this did not seem to faze the two newly born beings. As Lapris approached, she observed the depths of the thicket and with a simple wave of her hand, the vegetation dispersed. Like a jagged stone through cool water, even the trees sank down into the grassy depths of the soil. This would be a feat of incredible magic for the most talented sorcerers, however for any being of the First Company, this was no different from penning a letter. As the last vines crawled back into the deep from whence they came, there seemed to be a figure who didn't belong to the ground but instead belonged to the same blood as Madness and Lapris.

"Hello, I'm Vespass. Hey, you guys are like me?" the mysterious man shrouded by trees said with such a confidence that it knocked Madness.

Inside the complex anatomy of Madness, deep inside the fabric of what he was, something changed at that moment. And thus, the feeling of anger was created.

Chapter 17

King in the Rough

Forcefully, the doors to the great hall were thrown open. Even the guards in the room felt my radiating anger seeping through the pores in my skin and festering in the old oak beams. The hilts of swords were gripped and eyes devoured by each stride I took towards Ichilla, seated on his throne again, his head reclined deep in a slumber or thought.

"Ichilla," I demanded his attention. However, unphased, he mumbled,

"John?"

"Where is he, Ichilla?"

Again, my demands met with nothing but silence, still in a trance by the whispers of his throne.

"Oh yeah, I forgot to tell you, we found the boy, but you were already gone. There wasn't much I could do," he said, as he finally opened his eyes which, as they met mine, quickly diverted before retreating to the simplistic thoughts that once inhabited his mind.

"Sir, we met a Mr Overmont and a shell of a child. He told us soldiers took Kolm," Estrilda mentioned stepping and naturally bending forward to a bow, her reluctance hidden behind her military form.

"Yes, that would be correct, 'General'. The boy is in the dungeons. Don't worry, we have the best exorcists in Amor Ceriel, perhaps even in freshwater too, they will deal with this beast."

"Ichilla, this is a beast, a monster, a virus and not a ghost or demon. The boy isn't possessed."

My words struck a nerve within Ichilla, who abruptly stood closing the distance between us and placing a firm grip behind my head.

"You have bigger problems right now, John…"

"Bigger problems?" I enquired, the evident confusion present within my questioning.

Ichilla gave a faint nod, an immense invisible pressure hanging over him as he turned unable to look at my eyes.

"The defeat of Burncorn at the Field of Emeralds has cloaked the rest of them in anger and aggression. They plot to meet our forces at Mortuorum."

"Who are 'they'?"

"All of them… a last attempt to eradicate their so-called oppressors. Thornfief and Freshwater. They long for the taste of blood."

Over the past months my bed had become less used for sleep and more commonly used as a place where I could let my thoughts wonder in safety without the disruption or anxieties, where spectators couldn't listen intently to my thoughts with a cupped ear. Thoughts of mine departed my mind like a rowboat from the dark depths of a cave, eerily dipping oars into the waters of wonder out into the open realms of possibility. It is with caution that these thoughts came to mind. I always was under the impression that a god or higher being could be reading my life page by page.

Comparable to a jester, I felt the invisible eyes of the beings on thrones, watching me and judging me… I could hear their silent mutterings and their incoherent tuts. I no longer felt the hero Ichilla portrayed me to be and instead I was no more than an apple in an orchard. A fish among many. Only I had the fluorescent scales, that attracted the light and moulded it into many gorgeous colours that bounced on the waves of the cold blue deep. But still, wounded by spears, hooked by fishing rods and eaten by predators. Still wounded by sword. On a field where our many fathers have fallen before us, my name was always to be written in blood where the jade blades of grass lay next to the crimson coated blades of steel that fell with the iron suits that wield them. War beckoned me. War integrated its way dripping through the cracks in my consciousness. Each drop like roots through soil, seething and searching its way through me. An inherited madness that refused to die, instead further pushing me on a path which I was forced upon, all while being told 'freedom' was always my choice. Madness spoke and whispered, and I could finally see that my story was approaching a finale. And like a Jester, I will bow in front of my unseen, invisible audience and pray that what I have done will suffice.

I walked along the upper levels of the hall of Amor Ceriel. I couldn't help but approach Ichilla, as I saw him admiring the empire of Amor Ceriel through the pane glass, the light painting his face in a rose light. The light seemed to cut around the sharp edges of his face and curve around the smooth parts. Ichilla was an odd man who seemed to have a sixth sense. Unaware where the many citizens who inhabited his kingdom, unsure if magic ran through the youthful veins of Ichilla or if a darker force was lingering behind his deep blue eyes.

"Are you ready for war, John?" he uttered, like a priest baptising.

"I'm unsure of life, Ichilla. The past months… they've been little more than a dream to me, albeit a bad one. There's an impenetrable fog that's rested upon my life – I can see little more than each step I take. A dense fog, in which I can see nothing."

"And does this fog bring fear?"

He turned from the glass, his tongue like a knife slicing through the air with a clean cut. The rose illuminated part of his face, the other shrouded in the dark shadows that crept through the corridors of Amor Ceriel, along with the other spectres. I felt his gentle voice grip me. His jaws clasping me as if a predator were unwilling to kill its prey, yet its sharp teeth dripping with the temptation.

"I fear all."

The statement left my lips like paper on the delicate skin of a finger. I knew that in admitting fear, I was indeed inviting it further into my being, beckoning it from the dark corners that I was unsure even existed. I felt a newfound fear in all, from the simple man, to the creaking woods where faces peer from behind the labyrinth of trees and the mocking giggles echo through the thicket into the forest of your mind. Fear encourages fear and likewise the fear of war, the fear of Ichilla and the fear of all, brings a descendent of the harrowing emotion to the forefront of my being. Madness and despair crept, treading lightly across the frozen lakes of thought, ever careful not to break the ice. Not until the time was right.

The night was painfully silent – the night before war. Ichilla, being the type of man he was, created a feast. All the best foods and beverages in the land were brought to Amor Ceriel. It was his belief that this would bring benefits in battle. That axes would swing harder and the sword would cut cleaner if bellies were full and ale ran through the veins of the knights. The men who would soon be shaking in suits of metal, huddled around the halls in their companies. I entered the hall to find the food cold, many pale faces unable to eat the meal provided. Estrilda's face held colour to it, a healthy glow that seemed to make Speak appear less tense as he stood next to her. I worked my way over to them, giving nods of kindness and appreciation to the other pale men on the way.

"John," she said, "you decided to come to this pre-war parade as well?"

Her utterings made it clear that she was as unimpressed as I was, perhaps because of how much of her persona had been moulded into a sword wielding warrior but most likely because she was just as afraid as I was.

"Yes."

The words managed to leave my mouth through my frantic nail biting and irregular breaths.

"We'll be all right. Foods pretty shit here anyways. You heard about Ichilla?" Speak said.

"About facing the combined armies of the 'free lands', yes, Speak, we were there," Estrilda snapped, as I observed the two bickering.

Butterflies swirled in my stomach and words refused to leave my mouth whenever they argued.

Forcefully, I managed to piece together an enquiry. "What about Ichilla?" I asked.

Speak turned to Estrilda who in turn, turned from him with a scowl.

"Ichilla won't be on the lines," he said.

"Course not; who else would keep that fucking throne warm for him?" her angry voice muttered, purposefully ensuring her words would reach as many ears as possible.

"I'm sure it will be okay," I said, my voice lacking optimism, instead shaking with an unknown anxiety.

Estrilda looked at me, unconvinced and let down. Perhaps she subconsciously had hopes for me as the 'saviour of the wildlands'. Perhaps her thoughts were even conscious, implementing her anger further. She walked towards the balcony. I hesitantly followed. Never before had I learnt about women, when to follow and when to not. Speaks face was not encouraging as I paced to the balcony of the hall where Estrilda concluded her retreat. The night was bitter – a dense cold ached the air and paralysed my lungs. The howls of beasts and the impish whispers of spectres emanated from the darkness outside the walls of Amor Ceriel, as I embraced Estrilda. I wanted to protect her from it all. In turn, I needed her comfort to protect me, a shell of emotion. The last night before war.

Chapter 18
The Silent Cries

Madness festers. Despair manifests. Misery prevails. The sleepless nights that haunted me as I stared emotionless into darkness. Yet a hurricane of darkness overwhelmed me. I had become a lost conduit of nothing and an embodiment of delirium. A deep frustration of the lack of contentment became apparent and I could not deny the impulse to destroy. Dreams had abandoned me and I was left with the harsh reality without dreaming. Without the dreams of returning to my home, without dreams of a future, a goal or a purpose. My head spilled with the repetitive stories and whispered of my potential that was written onto the planes of reality with chalk. Easily faded. I felt myself losing control of the reigns, as the horse begun to buck and revolt. Control distorted and shifted. Shouts and screams built inside, screams of frustration in a rage of anguish. And when I finally opened my eyes to reality once again, I saw the destruction of what used to be the chambers I stayed in. Walls torn and splintered. Novels torn and the paper littered my floor. On my knees I perch in my room with bleeding hands that were never designed for violence. Tears and blood become one, knowing that when the sun rises in its endless cycle, so did death.

That morning the wooden door, dented with knuckle deep rivets from the previous night, felt especially heavy. I left the room with a heavy body and a fearful heart. Fate had predetermined the course of the days and nights to come, however the thought of a silver blade carving through my shoulder made my hair stand on end. The breakfast hall that morning was laid out beautifully however I imagine no knight fully appreciated the gesture from Ichilla, who sat overlooking it all. I sat near Estrilda and Speak. They were in my company; if we were to die today, which we sincerely believed then at least it would be amongst friends. My stomach grumbled the loudest grumble. I could not even bear the thought of consuming any of the delicacies placed symmetrically on the long table. I was far too prepared for war; I was certain I could even smell the metallic smell of blood on soil. My wobbling knees shook the table, only slightly, just enough for the surface of the water in a glass to ripple.

Unwillingly and forcibly I said, "Morning, Estrilda."

Her head did not swivel and respond with a kind yet reasonably harsh comment like usual and instead a slight nod of acknowledgement was all I would get from her.

"She's all right. Think she's just trying to block everyone out," Speak said.

"How are you doing?" I enquired with Speak through my ritualistic nail biting.

"Been better. Didn't sleep much."

He nibbled on a piece of bread like a rabbit would, the crumbs sprinkled on the table. After the meal (or lack of) Ichilla nodded in agreement with the whispers of his throne, before rising to talk.

"Knights. The neighbouring villages threaten Amor Ceriel. They lack the faith and knowledge to understand. It is this great city that will bring prosperity, peace and justice to this country. John Sawyer! He is the saviour of the country and of Amor Ceriel as foretold in the whispers of the throne. With him, losing is mere fiction. We breed an army who fears no evil; march with valour!"

I cast my mind back to when I was a boy. Couldn't have been any older than ten. It was a frosty morn on Handsel Monday. I could remember waiting at home in anticipation. My father had left when the suns light first reached the edges of the house, leaving a damp residue from the frost and few flakes of snow. This damp eventually accumulated at the foot of the house creating a puddle around the abode which I pretended was a moat. The damp infected the wood of the house, occasionally creating a moss encouraging all sorts of beasties into our home. The hinges on the door were cursed with a very distinctive squeak which meant I always knew when father was back. On this morning, the squeak rang throughout the house and I ran to the door to greet him, though he hadn't been long. In his arms he cradled a cloth which coated another item. He crouched down and ruffled my hair with his hands which were large enough to cover my head entirely and he then pressed the item into my hands.

"Carefully now," he said sternly as I unwrapped it from its cloth prison with haste.

I can still remember the feeling of joy and excitement I felt as my hand gripped the hilt of the wooden sword that presented itself to me. It was heavy and had little chips missing from where it had been bashed about, likely in father's firewood trailer, but that didn't matter. It was mine.

My very own sword. I imagined being on top of a mountain, as a snow wyvern gnashed its teeth and I would wave my sword and leap to conquer the beast. Of course, in truth I was simply standing on a chair, proclaiming to kill a snow wyvern to an empty room, but such is the imagination of a child. I believed that battle was such an invigorating act, that slaying an evil beast or bringing justice through steel was what it meant to be a man. Father had always told me how one day when I was big enough, I could have my own sword, a proper one made from the iron found deep in mountains and crafted in the heat of a dragon's breath. And so, I dreamed of the day when I too could go on quests alongside father, both brandishing steel, slaying beasts and righting wrongs. Righting wrongs.

My boots squelched through the mud. The viscosity seemed unusual for it had not rained the night previous. The armour seemed heavier than last I remembered in the Field of Emeralds. It clanged more and caused the chainmail underneath to graze my skin with each step I took. I spent some of the journey trying to bring ideas forth for the benefits of ditching the armour entirely. It was those little arguments I had with logic in my head that kept me busy in times like that. Occasionally I would spot an earthworm or a ghastly figure on the horizon and it made me question if I would end up eaten by the earthworm and forced to wonder the plains as a spectre, till the sun rose no more. I always heard that ghosts were not friendly. It did seem an awful long time to be alone, long enough to drive anyone crazy. Was madness festering in them, nailed to their bones with a rusted pike like it was in mine? Questions boiled inside me like a warm stew on a cold day. It was these questions that distracted me from the imminent massacre. We were called to a halt with Estrilda demanding our company to seize marching. Speak stood nearby. Strangely, despite wearing armour, he still seemed tall and lanky and his armour clanged half as much as mine. I saw him gripping his sword and his compressed face sweating in his helmet. I too gripped the hilt of my weapon, expecting an ambush or an immediate call to charge.

Instead, I heard Estrilda mutter quietly, "Let them pass."

I peered over her shoulder, keeping quiet, except for my broken rhythmic breathing. I saw a crowd of faded people walking across the field into a dark wooded area. They were translucent enough to see the dim green of the grass through their torso, yet if you squinted you could see them, dressed in older colourless tunics.

"What are they?" I heard Speak utter, for he too was peering over my shoulder.

"Empties," Estrilda said.

"Empties?" I reiterated. My repetitive response did not warrant an answer from Estrilda who remained silent until the translucent figures had all been cloaked by the shadows of the forest.

"Rise," Estrilda said, and just like that, the company stood and marched without question.

Empties. I remember Father mentioning the word once, but didn't remember the meaning, or what they were. *Must be something to do with witchbloods,* I thought. Perhaps it may relate to Cassandra Boyle? I did not know. What I did know is that that life was behind me. I was not the foreign adventurer from strange lands. I was saviour of the wildlands appointed by Ichilla.

"Estrilda, what are empties?" I whispered over the drums of marching and the drone of metal armour.

"Ugh. Empties are the emotionless entities left over from a dead body. The emotions are taken by witchbloods. They tend to use them for shells and that. Disgusting creatures, they are."

Shells? Empties? It all seemed like an ocean of confusion to me, one that I was not willing to dive in to just yet. My vacant attention was then abducted from the safety of my questions and wonderings by the distant battle cries of the 'free'. Immediately I began to ask myself if they were really free? If this war would free them or if freedom was even real, but I quickly digressed. I heard Estrilda's quiet prayers as she drew her sword. Her blade was skinny and appeared feeble. Of course, this perception was inaccurate, for on the Field of Emeralds she swung it gracefully carving her way through the enemy lines. Without hesitation I grasped the leathered grip of my weapon and drew it. The noise of the crowds of steel leaving the sheathe was one that inspired fear and anxiety, yet bravery. And when faced with death, men can only shout. A shout that brought forth all the pain, worry and anger. A shout that became a scream. A shout that held so much integrity and emotion that you could feel the air carry a sea of feeling. Then began the charge.

Chapter 19

The Procession of Blood

The cries halted and was replaced with the sounds of thudding boots on the mudded fields. It was eerily quiet during the charge, most notably was the noise of my erratic breathing through the steel slits in my helm. The first suit approached, swinging without thought or technique. Wild and animalistic swings. Patiently I waited for my opening and swiped through his midsection. I didn't wait to check if I had killed him – I saw red spray from the rivets in his armour and that was good enough for me. From the corner of my flinching eye, I spied armour bearing the Amor Ceriel insignia, tall and lanky I suspected it were Speak. He too crashed through a suit taking a few glancing swings on his chest plate. The sky was grey – too grey. Death loomed over the battlefield, sharpening its glaive with its bone finger. Clouds felt the overwhelming presence of death which coated them in shadow and darkness. I saw another suit of armour and this one was more sleek and agile. Estrilda had many quiddities about the way she fought and her elegant way of painting with the blade was almost artistic. And suits would fall as they approached her; the steel was lightweight and she whipped it around at such speeds, it was neigh impossible to fend off. Swords recoiled off mine and I felt the tremors deep in my bones followed by an underlying ache that built. I was unsure if it were fatigue or perhaps my bones had finally splintered. With festinate movements, we proceeded through the opposition. There were an extensive number of them and the pressure was immensely uncomfortable. An oppressive feeling of overwhelming numbers made thoughts of fleeing present themselves from the depths of my mind.

Shouts, cries and screams echoed through the gaps in the rain as a storm cascaded down upon us. The feelings of fear and helplessness begun to hiss in my ear like a snake on my shoulder. Thunder boomed, mocking the comparative silent cries of men as they fell to their knees with their own blood staining their clothes. The haste of men as they scrambled to dismiss their instincts of fear, forcing their right hand to raise and swing their swords once again. Dark shadows branched over the coarse soil, like fingers of twilight demons, inching closer, scraping on the lifeless and soulless bodies that lay cold. The bright light emanating from the lightning, meant that for a split second you could look into the eyes of the enemy. And see the eyes of sons, fathers and brothers, as the concept of a man is shattered like glass, each fragment ground into the negative emotions that bred tears. The tears that were more than just salt and water. Tears that held the deepest emotions brought to the surface through the slaying of another, through madness, fear and despair. The obtuse feeling of the compressing soul as its crushed by the self-provided thoughts of loathing. Slowly it becomes nothing and little more than human instinct to survive.

I felt the patter of rain as it dampened the ground with which my boots were planted and glistened along the surface of my armour. I felt it run down the crevasses and grooves of the armour and I felt the descending presence of madness as it began to convince me of the ways of blood, anger and resentment. The nihilistic thoughts embodied themselves in my being. I felt a violence I hadn't felt since that day on the Emerald Fields. I felt my fingers constrict around the leather handle, I felt my teeth grind and my vision engulfed by a darkness that had the hunger to kill and the urgency to harm. I felt an ancient madness possess my emotions, imprisoning logic and empowering the reckless nature that dwelled deep within the caverns of my mind. I was unseeing and unknowing of my actions, in a pool of thought, distant from reality. The reality of blood coating my sword, different shades of crimson and rose from the men of the 'free' neighbouring villages, who were unknowing of the madness that was soon to descend upon them. The aggressive vibrations of clashing steel shook my frame. An ancient emotion possessed my being. The descending of darkness inherited my muscles, as I became less human and more of a convulsing vessel, made of flesh and blood, carrying the purest form of madness. The lightning crackled, illuminating my blooded blade, the script deceivable and no longer was I bound by the words of man. Sword swings became nothing but a blur of rose and with haste the enemy would feel the steel as it gleaned through the hull of their armour and seared though their flesh. I would move without hesitation. Without fear. Halt would not stop the procession of blood as I led the knights of Amor Ceriel.

Deep cries from souls as they descended into the cold and the endless abyss of death silenced the battlefield. No man remained victorious. The weary fell and the strong fell further.

Dark skies prevailed, as the sun's rays struggled to reach the land. Rains from the north fell like tears and the thunderous cries boomed, crashing around the mountains before waking me up from my slumber from reality. Upon a mound of corpses, I stood, the shade of mercy absent from my blade.

Chapter 20

Peace

The memories of battle never dimmed from my mind and the fresh colours and ambience remained bright as ever. The Empire of Amor Ceriel had become seemingly all powerful, with the itching youthful fingers of Ichilla spanning all of the country. The remains of the free villages buried their dead, however some decided it be better to let the unforgiving force of time erode and rot the dead. Many feared the battle site, claiming that there was so much death, even the once green grass begun to lose its colour and die. I remember sitting with Ichilla in my chambers post war.

"We did it, John. We saved everything. The country, Amor Ceriel. Everything."

"At what cost? The massacre of all else?"

We were never to see eye to eye on the matter.

Ichilla, agitated, responded, "We did what had to be done. You've fulfilled your prophecy. It's time to rest."

And so, I did.

A cycle had passed and winter had wrought it harsh weather upon the land before leaving it to flourish as colour inked it once more. A land far in the west over the mountains of Caladrius (which all seemed like a faded memory now) bore fruit so sweet and nutritious it was said to have been given from the gods. My latent feelings of attraction to Estrilda blossomed with the seasons and we sought this land. By the time winter was to bring the bitter cold again, we would be sheltered in a cabin, built from wood by hands too battered for war. Speak stayed behind at Amor Ceriel insisting that if he wasn't going to keep the place in check, who would? We missed him. The cabin was erected in the field near a lake that trickled down a narrow rocky path and as the sun set it would glisten the water to appear as diamonds. A deep wood thicket surrounded the field of lush grass where we chose to reside. The wood was a golden brown and was polluted with that soft earthy smell. Seeds floated on the wind, navigating through the wood as the sun's rays broke through the treeline lighting the mossy undergrowth. Estrilda soon softened her persona, becoming less of a war general for the most powerful Empire in the country and instead becoming a woman who I learned to love.

The morning was bright – our petite room lit by the rising sun. I turned to Estrilda who lay asleep next to me with her brown hair floating delicately on the bed. Sleep in this land was deep, no sound of beasts, nor a threat of war. Slowly I rose from the bed careful not to awaken the sleeping woman. My shoulders ached and the aftereffects of war never left my side as did the memories. However, in this land, with this life I held with Estrilda so dearly, I could put the thoughts and flashes of death aside. I found a very slight chill in the house. The first sign that winter would soon rise from its slumber. I found my coat, made from deer pelt, hung on the back of our door and I left to the open field, briefly looking over my shoulder to see Estrilda still deep in her subconscious. The cold was refreshing from the warmth of my coat. I moved towards the wood, axe in hand and the crunch of frost under my boots. The fireplace in the cabin engulfed wood by the tree, yet somehow there always seemed to be more fuel nearby. The trees had a gentle sway but I felt no wind on my face. The cold ached my brittle bones as the axe raised and made a splintered cut into a trunk. Youth was leaving me despite of me being youthful and the pain never left my body, despite my absence from the battlefield. I felt the presence of wood life surrounding me and observing me as I chipped away at the tree. Dragging the wood back to the cabin was tough on my wobbly knees – though it wasn't too far. Soon I found myself out the wood and in the clearing where myself and Estrilda were living. A thick fog streamed from the chimney and tainted the clouds into a light grey. Estrilda had evidently awoken and was burning the last of the wood to remove the chill that inhabited the home. I slowly creaked the door open, attempting to drag the wood inside without the door swinging shut, trapping the load between the outside and in.

"We're almost out of wood," Estrilda mentioned, not seeing my struggle.

"Yes," I growled.

She stopped tending to the flittering fire and turned to the doorway where I had been stationed for an oddly long time.

"Ah," she said, filled with pleasant delight before jumping to her feet and helping me bring the wood inside, and piled it neatly by the fire. "I didn't hear you leave this morning?" Estrilda asked.

The house was silent and filled only by the quiet pops and crackles of the fire.

"You were asleep, deeply. I felt the chill of winter."

"So soon? Could that much time have passed already? Only feels like a few moons ago we were banging nails into the beams of this house," she said.

She stood, while I piled the last few wood blocks and she began to prepare a cuisine in the adjacent kitchen. Estrilda was as talented a chef as a knight. Though somehow, on occasion she would create a meal so rancid, I struggled to keep it down. Most of the time… she was a great chef. Today was one of those days as a delicate scent of cooking meat and seasoning filled the home.

"How did you sleep?" she shouted from the room opposite.

I grunted in response. "Still struggling?" I took a few seconds to compose a response with which she would be content.

"Sleepless. Just a bit. My body aches with my mind. Ah well. Not to worry."

"Well, no, it is still a concern. I've never seen anyone struggle with war like this."

I felt Estrilda's cold and freshly washed hands caress my shoulder.

"It's not just the war."

"What is it, John?"

I hesitated, reluctant to let her caring nature into my negative thoughts. I didn't want her concern, in this home and in this land and I didn't want any concern or fear. Only the rest and peace we longed for. I longed for.

"It's this feeling I can't make disappear. A lingering thought that won't leave. Ugh, if only I could speak with Caladrius."

"Caladrius? Who's Caladrius?"

"Just a friend."

Rain fell. Not the sort of rain that you dread and watch from your window with despair. It was the rain that fell through the sky with such grace and splashed on the ground with such finesse that it was mesmerising. A rain that captivated the mind as it did the eyes filling it with translucent colours and a rejuvenation that could not be found through any other means. A fresh rain that blessed the land with vitality, as the green shoots and roots coiled and curled, drinking, breathing in life from the ground. Rich soil writhed, as moisture sunk its way deep into the underground where no light would ever see. The patter on the roof was not an irritation; instead it became a meditation and a sound with which a rhythm would form. And a song would be created from the simplicity of rain, within which a particular beauty resided and would show itself in such an artistic way that it would make the greatest painter look like an ape drawing in mud. It was only then in that place, that I truly learned to understand the artistic force of nature. How the tweeting of birds was a tune that coincided with the whispers of the winds as they brushed the autumn leaves from the grasp of trees. Nothing but the brightest colours illuminated from the simple grass to the sky which was the bluest of all blues. How the splashing strides of water down a narrow stream could hold so much more beauty than the eye can see. The sounds as it crashed from stone to stone and the sun gleaming through the transparent waves refracting into sparking rainbows etched within the water. And a parched foul would emerge cautiously from the thicket and on shaky legs, walk to the stream to lap up the refreshing water. The breath of the animal would deform the water into different shapes indescribable to man. Such creativity nature held, unseen and unappreciated by any. I learnt to see what before was unseen, a world with which I could be content. One with Estrilda by my side in a place of peace. Contentment was found there, deep in the soil and earth. A contentment I could not discover in myself even as a child. Only now, after visiting this strange land, fighting in wars where I killed men who were friends. After living in a nightmare, I finally found contentment.

The sun fell, bathing the clearing in a tangerine glow. Estrilda and I sat near the stream, the water whistling down the rocky path and we admired the beauty of the life we created for ourselves. We laughed as people do and talked as people talk. Questioned as philosophers would. Before long Estrilda posed a question to me.

"Hey, now I've got one for you. Why do you think the sun rises each day?"

"I'm not sure. Perhaps it has a fascination with the land? Wants to see it often."

"Maybe," she said snuggling up to my side, "or maybe… it's chasing the moon?"

"Don't be stupid." I laughed.

She grinned too. "I'm not!"

"What happens when the sun realises that it will never catch the moon?" I asked smugly.

She paused for a moment as we both stared at the last few seconds of light as it faded into the horizon.

"Well… let's just hope the sun never realises that," she answered. "Sometimes, it's best not knowing."

I shrugged my shoulders. I hardly disagreed with Estrilda. She was right about most things. However, it was her lack of yearning for more knowledge I could not understand. A deep thirst had worked its way into my being and one that I couldn't deny. I had to know why. Why I felt an unrecognisable feeling despite the peace in which I found myself? Why Ichilla let me leave so easily after fulfilling the prophecy? Could the wildlands really be pure now? A safe haven? Could I really have brought peace and prosperity to the land? I needed answers. I needed to know why.

Chapter 21

The Glass Lake

"John, you promised," Estrilda said with a motherly warmth in her voice. I tossed and turned with angst, reluctant to listen to her words. An unexpected moan left my mouth before sitting up and squinting at the bright room.

"I know, I know," I uttered.

I caught my reflection in the mirror and stared at the grey in my beard and the caverns of wrinkles in my skin that had begun to protrude from my face. I stared at a man I did not recognise, yet who I'd come to know. I left the comfort of my bed to greet Estrilda in the living room.

"Dad!" a young voice called throwing his arms around me, gleefully with such innocent joy. "Can we go fishing now? The lake has thawed since dawn."

"You've been watching it, Cal?"

"Of course!"

The eyes of a child are ever observant and eager to learn for that is human.

"You said you'd take him," Estrilda mentioned, ruffling the young boy's hair.

Of course, I had every intention to take him. Perhaps it was my lazy demeanour or poor posture that hinted less.

"Yes, Estrilda. Let us prepare. Cal, get the rods from the shack."

Without hesitation or complaint, he bounded for the door, which he only cracked open slightly and slid his fragile physique through the doorway and out to the shack.

"It'll make him happy. You know he wants to see the fish," Estrilda said, affirming my decision to embark on the trip to the Glass lake.

"I know," I said.

"Are you okay? Unknown thoughts have been on your mind. Don't keep them secret."

"I'll survive."

I forced my feet into my old trekking boots which was slightly degraded from years of use. My shoulders rolled; still present was the shock from sword blows, clashing steel and heavy armour. Painful reminders of the past. I sighed and left the house – not a word to Estrilda. She couldn't understand my feelings. But she could be dragged into the madness that once inhabited me. I dreaded it.

The glass lake recently thawed and glistened under the warm sunshine. My son, Cal, ran to a nearby rowing boat, one that we had used before and attempted to push it out into the deep blue lake.

"Easy now, not too fast," I said, assisting his struggle.

His grunts and my exhales of effort lead to the boat leaving the bank and rippling out to the deep waters. I leapt in tugging my son by his collar onto the boat with me.

"Do you think we'll catch anything?" he asked.

"Perhaps. It is early."

"Probably not like last time huh? We got that giant carp. Remember?"

I grinned at the fond memory. It didn't seem to distant, though it was a year ago when he turned ten. We were out over the centre of the lake. I had to cast for him as he was never the best at casting out.

"Dad?" he asked.

I turned to him. "Yes, boy?"

"Mum was telling me of Amor Ceriel. The empire city? You used to live there apparently."

"Yes. Years ago. A year before you were born."

"Wow. What was it like? Were you a soldier? Did you know Ichilla?"

The inquisitiveness of the young lad brought back the dark memories of the past.

"I've buried that past, lad," I said morbidly.

"But it still happened? Can't you tell me anything about it?"

"Its… not like this land. This land is different. Safer. Brighter."

I held back from telling him all the truths of Amor Ceriel and the neighbouring villages. He was young.

"Huh. So, this is like being in a different world?"

"Guess you could say that. It's all just a bad dream now. A memory."

"Suppose you could call this a good dream then!"

I looked at him grinning with optimism and happiness flooding from his little green eyes. His rod twitched.

"You've got a bite, Cal."

He span around wrestling with the rod against the fierceness of the unseen fish under the surface of the water. Until the line went limp.

"Ugh, damn." He sighed as he sat back in the boat.

"Come on now. Let's try again."

He smiled as I cast the line out again. The line rippled in the water from his rod and mine. Both ripples bouncing off each other creating an equilibrium across the cyan blue surface. I could just about see fishes underneath the water, gracefully swimming and contorting underwater shifting directions and just brushing the dirt at the bottom of the lake. It was called the glass lake because every night, the lake would frost over. Even if it were a warm summers night it would frost without fail. Now many would consider this to be a bad thing as a thick sheet of ice would form across the lakes surface. However, when daylight came, it would be beautiful. The sun's rays would beat down on the ice breaking it into glistening shards that shone on the lake creating a sparkling wondrous sight. The glass lake was shining with beauty and wonder with all the colours of the rainbow underneath the new dawn sky.

Cal slept soundly that night. I laid next to Estrilda; both of us in silence.

"What's going on, John?"

"It doesn't matter," I responded, turning from her.

I was hoping that would perhaps end the conversation, but she was persistent, like the soldier she was all those years ago. The words of Cal stuck in my mind as well as their implications.

"Is this just a good dream?" I asked.

"Of course not," she said reassuringly.

"Why would you say that?"

I turned back to her; her hair flowed so effortlessly down her shoulders. It was beautiful.

"Just seems too good. I'm still fearful. But there's nothing to fear."

"There isn't a reason to be afraid, John. We're not in Amor Ceriel anymore. We're far from the empire. Why should you be afraid?" she enquired.

She was right and I knew she was. I turned from her again and she laid down snuggling underneath the blanket.

"Cause, eventually, you have to wake up… even from the best dreams."

Chapter 22
The End

It took more effort than usual to hack down the pride of the tree in the shrubbery that day. More harsh swings of the axe. I should've intuitively known something was wrong. A slight grey inhabited the grassland as the sun hid behind the cloud line. The familiar gentle summers breeze mutated and manifested into a harsh bitter wind. The wind chilled me even so while I wore a fur garment. I knew something was wrong. I felt my hairs stand; I felt a sickness in my stomach. A weakness inhabited my body and infatuated my thoughts with negative ideas. The axe left my weak grip; as the first flakes of snow began to fall, with haste I ran. Tumbling down the incline, my feet catching bristles and branches, falling to my knees, but the mere thought of the despair of nothing made me run. My shoulder came in contact with the door splitting the wood from its hinges. The house was dark. It had never been dark before. Estrilda and Cal… had gone. Left. My heart sank further into an abyss of decay. My breathing became rigid and distorted and I shook vigorously with fear and anxiety. The constant state of being afraid haunted me once again rearing its head from the shadows. Tears fell from my face contorted into a mirror of fear. And a voice from within me screamed. Not a cry of sadness, but a cry of pain, fear and desperation. Desperation that this reality in which I found myself wasn't real. That this was a mirage from a witchblood or a nightmare inspired by the devil. My cry echoed through the empty dark rooms swiftly followed by my blubbers of a fractured voice through tears. Through blurred vision I looked to the dark doorway where memories of Estrilda and myself resided. Memories of happiness now shrouded in misery and pain. From the doorway emerged a figure absent from sight due to the tears streaming from my face.

"Little, John, little, John. It's been a while. Sorry for the delay."

A woman's voice.

"Estrilda?" I thought out loud.

No, Estrilda's voice was so gentle, so innocent and so kind. The voice sounded similar to that of a bird I met long ago.

Confused with the transpiring events my broken words formed. "W-Who are you?"

"Think, John," she said kneeling, her finger lifting my chin.

Realisation fell upon me. Could it be?

"Cassandra... Cassandra Boyle," I said.

The witchblood from years ago.

"Hello, John," she said, a grin being pulled across her face.

Despite fighting in wars, despite bearing steel and slashing through men I was always terrified. A deep fear always resonated in me. Never was I violent unless the madness dawned upon me. At that moment in time, when Cassandra Boyle stood over my crying weak body, Madness

168

had a firm grip on me. Sadness became anger. Fear became insanity. Despair became a seething hate. My shaking broken body became fuelled by an unbreakable will of rage. Everything that brought me contentment after the horror of war, Estrilda, my son, this land and my home. All diminished with the presence of Cassandra Boyle.

"You took it all from me!" The words left my gritted teeth.

"Oh, come on, John; I'm not that childish. They left of their own accord."

Her patronising tone and the confidence of playful joy that emanated from her body further fuelled my anger. The madness festered in my heart. I launched towards Cassandra, my thoughts telling me to beat her on the floor till she didn't move. However, Cassandra was a witchblood and a powerful one at that. I leaped through her as if she were a shadow and I crashed into the log walls.

"Don't be so primitive, John. I'm just here to talk," she said.

I grunted in acknowledgement; the air left my lungs after leaping into the wall foolishly.

"Now, cast your mind back years ago. You remember that? You were looking for me, were you not?"

"Yeah… Tirynn told me you were dead."

"Were, John. I was dead. But like how you left Scotland, death can be left."

As I struggled to my feet, she watched, playing with a blade she found on the table. Her masochistic tendencies showed and I wasn't going to entertain them.

"Why are you here then? If you didn't come here to kill Estrilda and…"

She sighed deeply. "I never came to kill your precious wife-thing or your offspring. Didn't you ever wonder why you were sent to find me?"

I cast my mind back. Years past since the war and even more since I left my home to find Cassandra.

"My father. He asked me to give you a trinket."

She sighed again. My lack of knowledge seemed to be an irritant to her.

"John, I just left death. Don't let your simple mind deceive you into thinking a Trinket would hold any value to me."

"Why was I sent to find you then?" I enquired.

Her playful behaviour dimmed.

"I'm sorry, John," she said, for the first time, sympathetic.

"I am a witchblood. I'm unsure how well versed you are with our type but we do live for an awfully long time. I remember way back when the Whispering Throne was first crafted and spoke its first wisdom. I remember when Caladrius was imprisoned within the wall. That's a lot of time. I got bored, John, so bored of living every day, living for what felt like an eternity. So bored of living alone. So, I began to craft and experiment with new magic. I spat into dirt and clay and made people. I took some of the emotions from the dead and created Shells. The people of clay. They were mine. But they weren't what I had hoped."

She begun to pace around nervously.

"They were too human. Not what I had wanted. So, I let them out into the world. To discover to prosper... to bring peace and prosperity to a new land."

I felt sick. My ears were deceiving me. She had to be lying.

"Your 'father' sent you back to me, John... my Shell."

I stood up, dizzy, confused and mad.

"No… no that can't be… Ichilla told me… Caladrius told me. I was meant for more; born to bring the new world!"

"You're just a shell, John. Created to be with me, a purpose you couldn't fulfil. So, you left to live a false life. You're no saviour, John. You're no hero. You were lied to."

"A… a false life? But I lived; I met Estrilda and I fought wars!"

She put her hands on my face and rested her head against mine. Her pale skin was cold and her black robes draped around my feet.

"And for what? You're clay, John. You're not real. You were bent to Ichilla's will. You became what he wanted you to be and not what you were. I know it's hard to imagine. But please. Come home with me, John. I can take away your suffering."

She took my hand gently and led me towards the doorway. I knew not how Cassandra was going to take my suffering away, but if she could end this madness, take away this anger, this sickening feeling of fear, then it was worth it… but not yet.

"Not yet," I told her.

She stopped. Her grip on my hand loosened and she turned to me. Her face a picture of curiosity, as a glisten of her playful masochism boiled to the surface.

"What is left for you in this world, John? What do you want?"

"Payment," my voice grizzled.

"Payment? Money is of no value…"

"No… payment for what they've done. Payment for what they've done to me. Payment in blood."

I slammed my fist to the floor and felt the bones in my hands shatter. Blood trickled from my splintered hand.

"So be it. But you'll always be mine, John. My shell. You know what to do John. It's always been inside you. No need to hold back now. Goodbye," she said as she became a part of the shadow that hung in the darkness of the room.

The room littered with memories. Flashing images of a past that I never lived haunted me. Estrilda. Her smile. Her laugh. Such innocence and beauty that caused me such rage and anger. She left. She abandoned me like the others. I flung wildly at the wall shattering the aged wood. This cabin meant little to me now. This place that was once a home had become a conduit for my worst nightmare. The end was on the horizon for me and the end of my suffering. But I held too much anger and too much fury to end now. Madness cradled me as I once cradled my son.

"Please…" My agonising voice said.

My tears soaked my grey beard, and my cries were unheard. "Please!" I shouted, crashing the chair against the window, which smashed with ease.

A gale carrying darkness on its wind, entered the house. The end is nigh. I had to make them see. I had to make Ichilla, Caladrius and Amor Ceriel; I had to make them all see what they had done. What they had created.

"PLEASE," I screamed as I fell to the floor for the third time pulling at my hair.

The wind became eerily still. And I felt a touch on my shoulders as I was shrouded with the darkness, the familiar presence of madness. I felt as my 'Shell' was diminished from its memories of happiness with Estrilda and my son. The first time I saw her. Her kind smile lit the room and I kept nervously locking eyes with her. She was so perfect in my eyes. They burnt within a fire inside me. An inferno of pure animosity. I felt as I became a being of curses. One by one they filtered into my being, becoming a part of my 'Shell' and everything I was. All the curses fed on my pain and my suffering. I was a vessel for all the curses of the land to prosper and thrive. And when I rose my head, I glimpsed at my reflection in the cracked glass. Tears of blood streamed from my face; a face that once belonged to John Sawyer. My skin was pale and scarred, not from a blade or steel, but from the unseen scars of agony and fear. I was the man of 100 curses. Each etched on my skin and deep in my being. And I had been wronged. I had been lied to. The City of Amor Ceriel would burn.

Chapter 23

Burning

My broken body, fuelled by the will of dark powers, staggered from our home across the plains. Blood seeped from my boots and left a blooded stained footprint in the muck and dirt. The moon had begun its rise into the depths of the night sky and with the dawning of the sun, more dark curses began to manifest within me. Amor Ceriel was an empire and one which I had helped birth. It bore some of the most trained and skilled knights from the country – a formidable army. I knew I couldn't burn it alone. However, the Whispers from the throne were drowned out now by new darker voices. I knew what I had to do. I knew what I had to become. I walked among the plains and through a familiar wooded area. To which I approached a tree wrapped in chains and wrapped around a man. A man who hadn't aged a day since I saw him last all those years ago.

"Ah crap, you frightened me good, sir!" he said cheerily.

His cheer seemed unbreakable until he saw my face. He saw the contorted mess of anguish and pain. He felt the overwhelming pressure of the curses I bared.

"Oh, shit, I remember you! Christ, what have you done!"

I ignored the ghost and continued to make my way to the place I was always destined to return to. Where madness was most prominent within me. Every step the grass became greener and a brighter and deeper shade of green.

"The Field of Emeralds," I whispered.

I overlooked the grounds where the grass had been torn, where blood spilt on the land and armour remains littered the floor with their skeletal hosts. The essence of battle was still prominent and the memories still felt very real. I reached out with my hand and heart and could feel the depths of emotion of the dead. The fear, pain and suffering that filled their emotional spectrum before a sword cleaved through them. I spoke with the pain that connected us.

"Freedom. You sought freedom."

The grass rustled, responding to my words, "Freedom from Amor Ceriel. Freedom from the life you keep waking to. Freedom from the fear that controlled you every time the sun rises and sets. The never-ending cycle of discontentment with this world we are forced to live in. I was betrayed like you. I was lied to by Ichilla the deceiver. And believe me when I say. He will not see the sun rise tomorrow morn! So, let me ask you, free the people of Thornfief, Burncorn and Freshwater. Are you dead? Or merely patient until the heads of the liars, betrayers and mislead, roll onto the blood-stained stone of Amor Ceriel!"

And with that, the latent dark curses manifested. They too felt the pain and anguish. And so, the skeletal remains of the Free Armies of the neighbouring villages began to rise. Dirt and mud cracked and broke, as the armoured dead stood from below and drew their rusted weapons. The stench of revenge rode on the wind, towards Amor Ceriel.

"Is this what you want, John? A war?" Cassandra's voice spoke like a whisper from behind me.

"Yes. They will see us march on the hills and they will know. They can flee or fight. They can attempt to stop us with steel and stone. But their blood will spill. They will know fear as we have."

And the undead, begun to rally and march upon the Field of Emeralds. Amor Ceriel, the beacon of hope and the prosperous empire had now become the epicentre of anger, hate and revenge. Like moths to a flame, the undead armies of the free villages marched with their screams and cries of war still echoing from their broken skeleton skulls.

The sun had sunk on the horizon. Amor Ceriel lit up beneath the stars and the full moon. The gentle yellow glow underneath the distinctive white lunar light. The sky was clear, no clouds painted the black canvas and a vivid absence of any sort of winged creature. It was quiet. Not a noise of a ghost or daemon. No howls of wolves or Celestial storms. Even the wind rested just above the grass and dandelions that swayed just enough to make it noticeable. It was a perfect evening shrouded in the unappreciated beauty of nature. The sort that Estrilda and I used to lay under studying the stars and waiting for the sky to become a deep blue as the sun woke.

I ordered a halt and the nameless soldiers stopped. I took one last chance to admire Amor Ceriel in all its beauty. A city in which I truly was birthed to become a false saviour. A city built on the lies and manipulation of Ichilla.

"Tonight, we avenge the lives we've lost. We show them the fear they showed us. We bring war."

The silence remained as undead knights cloaked in darkness charged the city. It was an attack fuelled by aggression. Violently their swords swung at the defenceless and unsuspecting. I paced through the stone streets of Amor Ceriel and through the chaos that ensued around me. Fires raged, the flames unable to distinguish between the innocent and guilty as it engulfed all in sight. The armoured skeletons swung their swords with pain in their empty eye sockets as if they were alive. A defence attempted to form at the keep of the city. A weak attempt to stop a being baring the weight of 100 curses. Knights of the city charged me, swinging wildly, erratically and fearfully. Their swords hit nothing but air, as I swiftly drew my slender blade and precisely sliced away the gaps in their bulky armour. I was a shadow, a ghost of fury that was unstoppable to the men of Ichilla's guard and unstoppable to all mortal men. Man upon man, I slew. Those who swung their sword would only get to strike once before my blade cut through them effortlessly and violently. Those who chose to run were running in fear. I was through showing mercy for the merciless letting the despicable live because of their terror. My sword cut their bond to the land of the living. I arrived on the mountain of corpses at the door to the Great Hall of Ichilla. I turned to gaze at the burning city before entering the halls to bring about the End. The great doors opened to my touch and slowly they grazed the floor of marble before revealing Ichilla sitting back in his chair. His face irritated me; his relaxed manner irritated me. I smashed tables and chairs in the great hall as I watched Ichilla squeal in fear as I gradually approached him.

"John?" he asked as my hands splintered the dining table.

"John, what happened to you?"

I stopped still. The rage stopped; silence blessed the hall.

"You... Ichilla the deceiver."

"Listen now; I never lied to you, John; w… we saved the wildlands and you fought the war…"

"The war? It was our war! My war! I fought and slaughtered for a lie!"

I could feel him squirm, fearful of what I had become, as I lugged my cursed shell towards him.

"It's over, John! Amor Ceriel has the lands, I have the lands. Stop this madness!"

"You lied to me, Ichilla. You took it all from me! You gave me a life and you gave me a purpose before stripping it all from me."

"And you believe that by cursing yourself, that by burning down this city with innocence, that you'll feel some resemblance of happiness? That you will avoid the end of your path? That you'll eradicate this… this pain that leads your life?"

I stopped. He stood from his throne, the whispers becoming more frequent and harsh. They were less of a whisper and more like voices now.

"You think I wanted this? You think I wanted… or even planned to burn this city down? No… no… I NEVER WANTED THIS, ICHIILA! I never asked for this."

"I gave you purpose, John! You were nothing but a mere shell before me!"

I had heard enough.

"It's over… tell your lies from your grave, swindler." I raised my sword, a thick black fog coating the silver blade. Ichilla raised his hands flinching away from the blade. Perhaps his fear convinced him that his actions may prevent the sword from taking his life. His fear lied to him as he had everyone else. I walked towards the door and towards the glow of the city consumed by embers. The moon had turned a blood orange and a thick smoke coloured the deep blue of the sky. I raised my fist gripping Ichilla's head by his perfect blonde hair – a picture of fear forever carved onto his perfect face. The ghouls and dead banged their shields and swords and their cries manipulated into an essence of laughter and glee. Revenge had served them well. The city burned in ruins. I dropped the head. Ichilla's head rolled down the stairs of the keep joining the corpses of the royal guard. I looked over the massacre. People I once knew, soldiers I fought side by side with, and all slain by my sword. Speaks body lay dead at the bottom of the stairs. I felt the depression but the madness was deep rooted now and I had to make sure Ichilla and Amor Ceriel had their 'payment'.

"Are you done now, John? Is your crusade over?" Cassandra's voice whispered again from my shoulder.

Her voice sounded bored, as if the amount of dead was no longer entertaining for her; she was a masochist after all but it seemingly bored her instead.

"No... one more journey."

The snow was melting and the white coating on the floor was becoming a grey ash that fell from the sky. Terragoth, my presence hadn't been on the mountain in plenty of years. I could still remember the way though clear as day. Left at the boulder, forwards and up the mound and then the cave was up the path on the right. The cave was just how I remembered it, and as I took my steps in, the familiar dripping noise echoed.

"You're here. That's gone quick," a familiar voice said.

"Caladrius... did... did you know?"

"... John?"

"Did. You. Know!"

"The path you're on was destined, John. I knew."

When I first arrived on the plains, Caladrius was the man I trusted. But he knew I would be like this. Cursed and with more blood on my hands than most men in their lifetime. Alone, lied to and betrayed.

"You… you knew? I was a shell. With no purpose and you knew? You could've prevented all of this."

"But would that have been right? You were destined to…"

"I was destined for nothing! I am nothing. I can barely say I exist. I will not be imprisoned by your destiny shit."

"You're not imprisoned; you're free, John. You were always free."

His words coiled around me like a python. I wasn't going to bend to his will. I couldn't. I had come too far.

"How am I free, when I was always going to become this?"

"Choices, John. You always have a choice… you have a choice now…"

I knew what he was talking about. I could feel it inside me like a parasite.

"Choices. I don't exist. My choices have no meaning."

"You can create your own meaning, John. You're a shell, but that's the beauty of it! You don't have to be bound or imprisoned. You have the choice now to break free from it all. You know what you have to do."

I felt sick to my stomach and unexpected tears built in my eyes streaming from my face.

"I never thought it would come to this."

"Me neither, kid. But here's to new beginnings. Let's get this done with."

And with those words he bowed his head. His body went limp in the wall as he gave in awaiting my choice.

"Goodbye, Caladrius," I said, raising my sword, like an executioner at the blocks.

"Goodbye, John Sawyer, old friend," he said.

I squeezed my eyes to shut tightly hoping it would all go away. I cleaved my sword down and I felt the resistance as it cut through the neck of Caladrius. And as I stumbled from the cave, the dripping came to a halt and there was now only the roaring of the raging fire. The burning of the land. The lakes boiled and the trees consumed in burning embers of revenge and fury. This was the end. I fell to my knees and the fire creeping all over the land.

"It's over," I uttered as the curses of darkness that consumed my broken aged body evaporated.

I could now rest. And the orange glow of the fire was joined by the glow of a new dawn – the rising sun. This was the End.

Chapter 24

New Life

The painter gently grasped the brush by the handle. Carefully, he dipped the tip of the bristles into the vibrant colours as the wonders began. He envisioned a forest. A thick wood – one inhabited by an earthy smell, with damp mud and moss that clambered up the bark of the tallest trees. With each brush stroke, he crafted a perfect vision of what he saw. He wanted the forest to be filled with life. He wanted the forest to be the kind where young children could search under logs and find all sorts of insects and creatures living in their own miniature world. Where rabbits created little homes in holes under the earth sheltering them from the rain and cold. Carefully he painted a nest in the tree. A nest where birds could arrive to see their hatched eggs and feed their flightless young. A river flowed through this forest. A light stream that curved and danced around rocks and stones elegantly falling down a small waterfall and crashing along the murky banks. He painted and became content with his work. However, he felt as though something was missing. A certain emptiness. So, he pulled up his sleeves and opened a new pallet of colours. These colours were darker with all different browns, greens, blacks and blues. And so, in a clearing in the forest he birthed a deer. A stag, large and heroic. A beautiful creature that stood with pride in this fresh and vibrant wood. The stag was a wonder. He envisioned how the stag would pace along the clearing of the forest in the dawn. The fresh daylight would shine through the green leaves of the trees projecting a light emerald glow across the undergrowth of even the darkest areas of the forest. The stag would be listening intently for threats, however, would only be greeted by the morning songs of birds. The songs would be those of joy and happiness as they fluttered around the treetops. The stag would walk across the grounds and approach a shrubbery and would eat the green leaves provided to him by the gracious nature of the forest. A bee would buzz by and land on a nearby flower rubbing its thorax into the pollen before yet again taking flight into the endless forest. And the stag would gaze up and watch as the bee flew into the air and disappear into the rays of sunlight. When the time came, the deer would decide to drink from the stream lapping up the waves of water that is fresh from the source and high in the mountains where snow fell from the clouded skies. The painter took a step back from the canvas and admired his creation. His art envisioned in his subconscious and expressed onto a blank canvas of nothing. When nothing existed, the artist created his own reality. One which he became content with. A forest of perfection. A forest with wildlife with birdsongs and a flowing lake.

And the sun rose on a new day across the black ash remains of the great plains. A single green leaf blossomed from the remains of nothing. A blank canvas was born. And life was born to begin again.